Holly-Jane Rahlens

Wallflower

Holly-Jane Rahlens

Wallflower

A Novel

Rahlens, Holly-Jane
Wallflower

First U.S. Edition 2010 by Berlinica Publishing LLC, 255 West 43rd Street, Suite 1012, New York, New York 10036

First published in German translation 2009
Copyright © 2009 by Rowohlt Verlag GmbH, Reinbek bei Hamburg, Germany

Original English text
Copyright © 2009 by Holly-Jane Rahlens

Cover design: Eberhard Delius; Cover photo: Heike Barndt
Printed in the United States by Lightning Source

ISBN 978-1-935902-70-6
LCCN: 2010912622

www.berlinica.com

For Noah. Of course.

Content

One

The Girl Who Lived in a Crack

The Wall's down and I'm stuck. It's always been like that. Not the Wall, of course. It only fell two weeks ago. But me. I've always been stuck. In a crack. And I can't get out. If someone ever decided to make a movie about my life, they'd call it *The Girl Who Lived in a Crack*. It's like that *Twilight Zone* you can catch in reruns on TV where this little girl unintentionally slips through a crack in her bedroom wall and her father goes in after her and finds himself in a fifth dimension, in a hazy, abstract place where space, shapes, sound—everything—are distorted. That's how I feel sometimes. As if I were wandering around, aimless and dazed.

It's no wonder I get lost a lot. I try to pay attention, but then I start wondering, for example, why there are so many pharmacies in Berlin, and before I know it, I'm standing in front of the German Federal Pension Fund Office on Fehrbelliner Platz and have no idea how I got there or how to get home. In tourist guides, they're always boasting that Berlin has a pub on every corner. Not true! At least not where we live. But within a five-minute radius of our apartment, we have at least *nine* pharmacies. Is this indicative of a city full of sick people? Or of healthy people? It can go either way.

We live in the Charlottenburg district, we being me, Molly Beth Lenzfeld, eleventh grader, and my father, Fritz Lenzfeld, theoretical chemist. Please, don't ask me what a theoretical chemist is. It's complicated—you don't want to know.

So I'm spacey, I get lost a lot, and I'm currently living in Berlin-Charlottenburg. But not for long. Tonight we celebrate Thanksgiving big-time with our American neighbor across the hall, Bo Brody, and his German wife, Edda, tomorrow I pack my bags, and on Saturday I jet home to New York. *Auf Wiedersehen*, German Federal Pension Fund Office!

My father—I usually call him Fritz—will be staying in Berlin until July. We came last August for a year. When I told him a couple of weeks ago that I wanted to go home, he asked me to give it another try, to hang around at least until Christmas. But I'm not buying. It's time to go home.

My older sister, Gwendolyn—who's thirty-one and waitressing part-time at a Mexican restaurant off the highway near Burlington, Vermont—will be keeping an eye on me in New York. Conveniently, she just broke up with her seventeenth boyfriend this year and is looking forward to the change of scenery. Besides, she says, she can write the Great American Novel anywhere, even in Manhattan. Fritz, who in rare moments can be funny, teases her and says that the Great American Novel has already been written by several before her, including Melville, Twain, Salinger, and Shakespeare—to name only a few. But Gwen just ignores him and asks for another loan until her book is finished. I laugh. Gwen has no idea why.

"Shakespeare?" I say. "American? A novelist?"

Gwen groans and socks Fritz in the arm.

I don't mind staying with Gwen in New York. She's a good sport and probably *will* finish her novel some day, but, frankly, we're not a perfect fit. She couldn't care less, for instance, about the number of pharmacies in Berlin. If she were here, she'd probably go out and count the pubs instead. I'm more of a homebody, whereas she's always dragging me places that I don't want to go to, to smoky art exhibition openings, or tattooists that brand her upper arm with the name of her fourteenth boyfriend this year, or to the top of the World Trade Center for an early power breakfast with boyfriend number sixteen.

I take after Fritz, whereas Gwen is like Leonora. Leonora Sophia Lenzfeld. It's a beautiful name, isn't it? That's my mother. *Our* mother—a stunner if you ever saw one. Gwen takes after her, and not only in the beauty department. Just like our mother, she makes friends easily, she reads poetry out loud, she prepares great mashed potatoes. And like Leonora, Gwen can also fasten her bra behind her back in one second flat. I don't know how she does it. Maybe because she has so much experience taking it off and putting it back on with the guys. I, in any case, fasten my bra in front and then twist it around my stomach to the back, and then I slip my arms into it. I suppose Gwen would teach me how to do it the right way if I asked her.

My mother, who was a dedicated high school teacher, definitely would have if she had lived. But she didn't. At least not long enough to show me. I had just turned eleven and was not yet wearing a bra when she left us. It was very traumatic. Her death, that is, not the fact that I wasn't yet wearing a bra. One morning after breakfast, she went to the doctor's with a stomachache, and when she came home for dinner, she had cancer. Of the pancreas. Four weeks later, she was gone. She was so busy making friends and reading poetry out loud, mashing the potatoes, and putting her bra on the right way, that she missed all the warning signs—not that pancreatic cancer has many. And not that they stick out like a sore thumb.

You can't believe how many people came to the funeral. There wasn't enough room for everyone inside the chapel, so they were piling up on the sidewalk, mingling with the shady characters hanging out in front of the off-track betting office two doors down. Leonora's homeroom class came: thirty-five tenth graders. The Korean green grocer on Broadway was there, my mother's Russian manicurist, and all of my sister Gwen's accumulated boyfriends from the years 1975–1984. There were many. Everybody adored my mother. Everybody. But no one more than I did. Except maybe Fritz. And Gwen. But I was only eleven. So naturally the loss was greater.

It's gray out today, like most days in November in Berlin, like a black-and-white photograph from the 1930s in one of my mother's old photo albums. Murky skies, bare trees, cobblestones the color of pumice and charcoal. Old ladies leaning on canes roam the streets bundled up in bulky gray woolens and fat brown fur hats. Sometimes a color floats by, a bright yellow mohair knit coat on a stately African woman, a royal blue poodle hat on a toddler in a stroller, an explosion of pink from heather bushes displayed at the florist's up the block. The yellow and blue and pink seem so incongruous, fake almost, as if small areas of the black-and-white photograph had been colorized.

Gray, murky, bare. That's how I envisioned Berlin one bright afternoon in New York last June when Fritz told me he had won the grant. We were at our favorite sushi place on Amsterdam Avenue near Seventy-third Street when he broke the news. I almost choked on my chopsticks. He might as well have said we were relocating to the far side of the moon, to Mars, or beyond.

12

Fritz is a kind father. He hoped I would see the year in Berlin as an adventure, would re-create myself in a new environment, experiment, take to Berlin like a match to a Bunsen burner. Well, he was wrong. He may be a chemist, but when it comes to me, he's out of his element. He worries that Leonora's death has locked me off from the world. He forgets that I simply don't embrace change. Period. I get stuck. And I did.

Berlin was doomed from the start.

I'm in a hurry. Thick wet drops of gray mush start to fall as I dart past the sidewalk snack stand and slip into a tunnel that leads to the S-Bahn, Berlin's elevated rapid transit train system.

It's freezing in the tunnel. I'm glad I put on my fur-lined boots, winter slacks, wool knee socks, lambskin duffle coat. I throw the hood back, though. I don't like how it flattens out my hair. I have a new cut, a short, curly, brunette bob with bangs. It works.

My breath is steamy. When I exhale, I faintly taste the coffee I drank just before I left the house. I hope I'm going the right way. I've never been here. I take the bus to school—the German-American school in Zehlendorf. And sometimes I take the subway to Fritz's office in Dahlem, where university buildings mingle with the sprawling villas of the rich. But I've never been on the S-Bahn. Fritz says that after the Wall was built, West Berliners boycotted it for three decades because until a couple of years ago it was operated by East Germany, by the Communists, even the stations in the West. It takes a while to figure out the logistics of the setup. And I thought the New York subway was complicated!

The smell of stale, greasy french fries from the snack stand outside trails in behind me, but mostly I'm smelling the detergent that has lingered on my freshly laundered clothes, on my underwear and my plaid flannel shirt. I noticed the scent when I ironed the shirt this morning, flowery-sweet and artificial. I'm very odor-sensitive, and I had to gag. But I put the shirt on, anyway. I needed to wear comfortable but warm clothes. I'm on a mission. Today, Thursday, November 23, 1989. To East Berlin. To be exact: to Greifenhagener Strasse in Prenzlauer Berg. To my mother's birth house. If I don't go today, when will I?

"Not much has changed since she left," Fritz told me.

Last August, shortly after we arrived in Berlin, Fritz went for a look. Without me. I stayed home and hid under the covers. I wasn't ready to go yet. Now I have no other choice because I'm leaving.

"It's falling apart—like most everything in the East," he reported. "The plaster on the façade is crumbling. You can see the brick and mortar underneath. The balconies look as if they're about to break off and plummet to the earth. It was odd. I felt like I was back in the middle of the war."

Fritz grew up in a small town in the province of Hesse. He, his mother, cousins, and aunts survived the war by the skin of their teeth. Some of the men, including his father, my grandfather, a Wehrmacht soldier, perished at the front.

Several years before that, some 400 kilometers away, Leonora and her parents, like so many Jewish families, fled Berlin. If they had stayed, they would likely all have been murdered in the death camps. My mother didn't know that then. She was only six and a half. Later, when she found out, she felt hugely ambivalent toward Germany. Maybe that's why I do too. But I think if she had lived, she would have come to take

14

a look. Eventually. Would have gone back to Greifenhagener Strasse. Like me. Today. Despite the mixed feelings.

I look to my right and try to imagine Leonora beside me: slender, tall (though not as tall as me), silver hair catching the lights. She was a fast walker. I was always slightly out of breath when I tried to keep pace with her. Sometimes she'd grab me by the arm and point the way. She had a wonderful sense of direction. And a very strong grip.

I dip my hand into my pocket and pull out my Berlin Transit Authority (BVG) map. Which train line do I take again? The West lines are in various colors. The East lines are all black. There it is. The turquoise line, the S3. I take it to the last stop, Friedrichstrasse, cross the border, then take a black line east, then another black one north. A thick gray border runs through the middle of the map. The Berlin Wall.

I slept through most of the excitement on November 9. I'm a very sound sleeper. I'd gone to bed early, around ten. The doorbell woke me up. It was Edda and Bo Brody, our next-door neighbors. And then Fritz knocked on my bedroom door and said the Wall was down and did I want to go downstairs and celebrate, perhaps take a walk with them?

At first I didn't know what he meant. What wall? There was a wall in our backyard where all the trash cans were lined up, but . . . And then when I understood that they were talking about *the* Wall, it didn't immediately strike me as quite enough of a reason to get out of my cozy bed for, at least not in the middle of the night. But when they were gone, I couldn't fall back asleep right away and I went out to the balcony and I could see the Kurfürstendamm and hear the noise, all the cars honking and the people whooping. And I thought, *Wow, the Berlin Wall, this is historic. Maybe I should be a part of it.* But the fact was, I didn't *feel* a part of it, so I went back to bed and slept through it until—

"Hey, Molly Moo!"

I twist around, startled.

It's Carlotta Schmidt, from my homeroom class. I said my good-byes yesterday. I never thought I'd see her again.

"Boo! Molly Moo!" she says. A drop of her saliva lands on the tip of my nose.

I hate it when Carlotta Schmidt calls me Molly Moo.

"What are *you* doing here?" she wants to know. The way she says it, you'd think there was a law against me walking in the S-Bahn tunnel. No matter what Carlotta says, it's always shrill and it always sounds like she's mocking me. She's a real nightmare, too, a cross between Madonna, the pop singer Olivia Newton-John, and the German TV Lotto hostess, Karin Tietze-Ludwig. She has Madonna's bod, Olivia's bleached blond perm, and Karin's blank smile. She dresses, though, like the hookers who descend upon the Kurfürstendamm after dark. That cracks me up. The Kurfürstendamm! The classiest boulevard in West Berlin! Imagine, if you will, prostitutes hanging out in front of Tiffany's on Fifth Avenue or strutting up and down with the monks past St. Patrick's Cathedral.

Today Carlotta's wearing a skin-tight, neon-pink tube dress that stops just above her knees, high-heeled, skintight black-patent boots that reach just below her knees, black tights, and a black leather aviator jacket with shoulder pads like a football player's. The jacket hugs her waist. She must be freezing her butt off. Good.

She smiles her Lotto hostess smile, and I see a smear of red lipstick on her front tooth. Well, let her walk around with lipstick on her teeth. I'm certainly not going to tell her.

"I have some last-minute shopping to catch up on," I say.

I'm definitely not telling her that I'm on a mission, that I'm going to Prenzlauer Berg. She'd find a way to use that information against me somehow. Although who knows why I care? I leave Berlin on Saturday, anyway.

"Love your boots," she says.

You see! That's what I mean! She's mocking me. She *hates* my boots. She wouldn't be caught dead in them. Even I don't want to be caught dead in them. They look like paratrooper boots. In fact, they *are* paratrooper boots. I bought them at an army and navy store downtown, near Delancey Street. When you have a size twelve shoe like I do, you can't always be choosy with your footwear.

That's another reason why Berlin was doomed from the start. I can't find a pair of decent shoes in this town. No one, absolutely no one, it seems, has big feet, not even the boys in my grade. Not that I ever look at them—the boys, that is. And not that they ever look at me. How could they? They only come up to my chin. I'm a big girl. Not heavy, mind you. Just tall. Very tall. Six foot one—and possibly still growing! Gargantuan feet, massive hands, substantial breasts. I am a tower, a mountain, a monster of a girl. If Hollywood ever decided to do a remake of the movie *Attack of the 50-Foot Woman*, I'd get the title role hands down: *Molly Lenzfeld—she was more woman than any man could handle.*

And if they ever did a movie about Carlotta Schmidt, they'd call it *Young Slut on the Loose: For the first time ever on-screen, the awesome spectacle of Carlotta Schmidt's mating ritual! See the boys drool. Hear their hearts pound. Smell their hormones cook.*

"By the way," says Carlotta. "I saw a shoe store with extra-large sizes. For extra-large women. They looked nice. In case you're shopping for shoes." Her tone has a definite sarcastic edge to it. Did she have to say "extra-large" even once, let alone *twice*?

"Oh?" I say, feigning interest.

"On Nürnberger Strasse. Or Passauer. Somewhere back there in Schöneberg."

I know the store. It caters to transvestites. I bet she knows it's a shoe store for queens. She's making fun of me again! The slut.

We're approaching the steps up to the S3. A sign reads "FRIEDRICHSTRASSE."

"I have to buy a ticket," says Carlotta. "Ciao, ciao."

Ciao, ciao—how phony can you get?

"Oh!" she adds. "I'll see you tonight."

"Tonight?" I say—a little rudely, I should add.

"At Thanksgiving dinner."

"You're going to be there?" I say, even more rudely.

Of course! Our neighbor Bo Brody knows her mother, Audrey Rockwell-Schmidt, an ex-pat who helps Americans with their tax returns.

Carlotta's face clouds up. "Well, excuse me for wanting to celebrate Thanksgiving!"

She swings around and makes a beeline for the ticket counter at the end of the tunnel. Good riddance.

I turn to the staircase.

Ciao, ciao. Jeez.

I start up the stairs to the S3 train.

Hmm. Maybe I shouldn't have been rude. Maybe she really *was* trying to be helpful. Maybe she *did* see a nice pair of shoes at that store and honestly thought they'd be right for me. Maybe I'm just reading her wrong. Rachel Schwartz, a therapist I spoke to a couple of years ago, said that I may sometimes misinterpret nonverbal signals.

Now I feel bad. I should have given Carlotta the benefit of the doubt.

I turn back around. "Hey!" I call out.

Carlotta keeps walking.

"Carlotta!"

She's snubbing me now, refuses to turn around.

"You have lipstick on your front tooth!" I shout over to her.

She still has her back to me, but she raises her hand above her head and gives me the middle finger. It's a nonverbal signal that even *I* understand. I shrug and climb the steps to the platform.

Well, I tried, didn't I?

Two

The Boy Who Came in from the Cold

I find a window seat in the train and settle in.

The S-Bahn looks different from the Berlin subway. The seats here are made of wooden slats. And very hard. In the subway, the seats are cushioned and upholstered in green naugahyde. An old lady is sitting beside me, with a Chihuahua, shivering, on her lap. I smell its fetid hot breath. The lady's coat is wet, and the wool smells soggy. The coat actually smells more like dog than the dog itself. A thin man of about fifty wearing a dark blue skipper's cap is sitting opposite me. I wonder why German men like wearing those skipper caps. I see a lot of them around. Maybe it has something to do with the German male's need to wear a uniform? The man is gazing blankly out the window, trying his best to ignore me, a giantess sitting practically on top of him. His briefcase is on the floor in front of him, so I barely have any legroom. A newspaper, the *BZ*, is on his lap, but he's not reading it. I can read the headline upside down: "BORDER CONTROLS IN-CREASE AGAIN." The East Germans are clamping down after two weeks of open borders. Fritz says now that the Wall is down, smugglers are on the loose. "What on earth do they want to smuggle?" Edda, Bo's wife, wonders. "Pickles from the Spreewald?"

A schoolboy is seated next to the man with the skipper's cap, maybe ten years old or so, with his schoolbag on his lap. In his left hand is half a sandwich, and with the other hand he's trying to write in a notebook with a fountain pen. Big loopy letters. His fingers are smudged with ink, and the page has blue ink blotches all over it. Is the boy coming from school? I look at my watch. It's 11:10. No classes today for me. My school has a long Thanksgiving weekend.

I slip the subway and metro map into my shoulder pouch and pull out my map of Berlin. The train's doors are closing, but a splash of neon pink suddenly appears and thrusts them back open. It's Carlotta "Slut" Schmidt. She plops down on the aisle seat to the left and across from me, next to a woman in a camel's hair coat absorbed in the weekly newsmagazine *Der Spiegel*, with a picture of Karl Marx on the cover. An elderly couple with a scotch-plaid shopping cart sits opposite her. The dog next to me yelps. Carlotta looks up and sees me. She bares her teeth to show me that the lipstick is gone. Then she pulls her state-of-the-art Walkman out of her bag and tunes me out. The snob.

I'd been out with her and her mother, Audrey, when she got that cassette player. We'd been to lunch and then shopping, and I remember regretting it. Girls and their moms make me blue. Which is actually an improvement over the first year or two after Leonora died. Every mother-and-daughter couple I saw I simply wanted to murder. These days they just make me want to crawl back into bed. And sleep. And dream. Although I can do without the nightmares, thank you very much. The other night I dreamed that Leonora and I went bowling together. The bowling ball got stuck on my big toe, and I had to walk around in it as if it were a shoe. Leonora finally managed to pull it off.

The train starts moving, and the little boy's pen slips, marking the page with another blotch of ink. He sighs, exasperated. Why do the teachers in Germany insist that kids write with a fountain pen? It seems so cruel. On the other hand, the boy does have his hands full. I watch him take a bite from his sandwich, and I realize I'm actually a little hungry myself. I should have brought a snack. Thanksgiving dinner is not until 7:30, and Fritz warned me that there wasn't much of a restaurant culture in the East. "If you're hungry and you see a restaurant, don't be choosy," he said. "Just go in."

I look down at my map. It's open to the Prenzlauer Berg district. I find U-Bahnhof Schönhauser Allee and begin tracing the route to Greifenhagener Strasse. But then I look up and sniff. Besides the smell of my own freshly laundered shirt and the dog's breath and the woman's soggy woolen coat to the left of me, I'm suddenly aware of an unpleasant chemical odor in the air. Disinfectant, I think, but not the chlorine-based type that tickles your nose and smells squeaky clean like a swimming pool. No, this smells . . . old and sweaty. Like . . . chemical-based barf.

The woman next to me bends over and puts her dog down. She's probably getting off at the next stop. The elderly couple sitting opposite Carlotta get up too, and Carlotta takes their window seat. Now she's sitting opposite the woman with the *Spiegel* magazine. Carlotta and I are both facing forward now, sitting at windows on opposite sides of the aisle.

Sometimes I wonder if I'm just envious of Carlotta. I make her out to be a snot nose, and she is, but I must admit she looks fabulous in those loud clothes of hers. And she's got style—even if it *is* a little on the vulgar side. Not that I don't. My style is just more classic (despite today's paratrooper boots). Carlotta attracts attention. My goal is to hug the corridors.

When school began at the beginning of September, I actually tried to be friends with Carlotta. She was my designated "homeroom buddy," the person appointed to initiate me into school life. But we never really took to one another—not like Martha Rosen and I did. I miss Martha, my best (and practically only) friend in New York. We've been cooking buddies ever since we were nine and took a baking course at the Ninety-second Street Y. Over the years it turned out that Martha is best with fish and veggies, and I with meat and sweets. We're a perfect cooking pair. We talk about opening up a restaurant after college and calling it My Best Friend's Kitchen.

Kitchens are my favorite rooms. I inhabit them like a chemist does her lab. I'm a reliable cook, very methodical, my measurements exact. I know that different ingredients react together in a specific way: dough will rise if you add this, milk will curdle when you do that, when you whip egg whites they stiffen. But I also know that once you understand the basic formula, you can adapt it, change it. A good chef is willing to experiment and learn from success and failure.

"She experiments so happily in the kitchen," I overheard Fritz say to Edda Brody this morning, "so why not in everyday life?"

I was in the Brody's kitchen preparing the turkey for tonight's Thanksgiving dinner so Edda could stick it in the oven while I'm gone, and Edda and Fritz were in the living room polishing her silver. She's a child psychologist, originally from Hannover, with a five-month-old infant. I don't know how she finds the time to host dinner parties.

"Fritz," Edda said, "no one needs to worry about a dead turkey's feelings. It doesn't mind being stuffed and basted. And the cook doesn't mind fumbling around in its stomach. Feelings are sticky. Molly understands that. She's wary."

Yes, I suppose I am. I've always had a hard time with feelings. They're messy. Figuring them out is a chore. It takes a while to sort through the emotions, name them, redirect them from my heart to my brain and back. And let me tell you: that doesn't help making friends any easier. Especially in Berlin. It's not the language. I speak German fluently, if with an accent. I just don't fit in. Period. That was acutely evident early in the school year when I went to a party with Carlotta. Everyone was hanging around getting drunk or high, dancing and necking, and taking turns locking themselves into the upstairs bathroom with someone else's boyfriend or girlfriend. I didn't necessarily mind *not* doing it in the bathroom, but it would have been nice if Carlotta or one of the girls would have asked me for the recipe for the kiwi cream pie I spent hours baking and they spent three minutes gobbling up. And it would have been nice if one of the boys would have at least made the effort to make me feel welcome and asked me to dance, even if they *were* shorter than me. It didn't even have to be a slow dance. And it only had to be once. But no. No one asked for a dance.

Okay. Rachel Schwartz, my ex-therapist, probably would have asked me why I didn't think to ask one of the boys myself if *he* wanted to dance. I suppose I *could* have asked one of them. And maybe he *would* have danced with me. And maybe I *would* have had a good time. Maybe I would have had such a good time that the whole fall would have been different and I never would have even thought to go back to New York. Maybe, maybe, maybe.

Well maybe he would have said *no* when I asked. Maybe he would have laughed at me. Maybe he would have looked at me like I was demented. It's my destiny. No one ever asks me to dance. If Hollywood ever makes a sequel to *The Girl Who Lived in a Crack*, they'll call it *I Was a Student Wallflower*: "The tragic true-life tale of an uprooted, shy and clingy girl destined to wilt before she blooms." That's me.

The train rolls into Savignyplatz. There's a hustle and bustle as passengers get off and on. Cold air streams into the car, but the overpowering disinfectant odor lingers. I open my coat and hold the tip of my flannel shirt collar to my nose as if it were one of those perfume samples they pass out for free in Bloomingdale's cosmetic department. Better to smell flowery laundry detergent than that repugnant antiseptic.

A swarthy-looking, heavyset man sits down in Carlotta's original seat, pulls a rosary out of his pocket, and lazily plays with the beads, his eyes fixed on a distant horizon. Carlotta is listening to music on her Walkman. I can hear it over here, a rhythmic *zsh-zsh-zsh*. It's so loud, the woman reading the *Spiegel* looks up and glares at Carlotta. But Carlotta's oblivious.

I'm about to dip back into my map of Berlin when a dark shape swoops through the door. It's a guy. A boy. Maybe eighteen, nineteen. He ducks so as not to hit his head on the door frame. Once inside, he stands upright. That's what I call tall. Titanic tall. Maybe six foot four. He leans back against the partition, wedging a huge shopping bag between his legs. He unbuttons his jacket and shakes off the wet. It's made of black leather and hangs loose on him. It looks a little worn, but you can tell it's a good swatch of leather. It has a vintage air to it, as if it were from the 1930s or 1940s. He's got a black T-shirt on underneath and a black vest over it. His jeans look a bit distressed; his boots are battered. They're like mine, like a paratrooper's. He runs his hand through his hair. It's wet,

25

messy, curly, dark. I notice a silver loop in his left ear. And he hasn't shaved. His cheeks are stubbly. He looks . . . tough. But in a gentle way. Our eyes meet. It's just for a second, maybe not even that. But I look away. It's too intense for me.

A moment later, out of the corner of my eye, I see him pull off his wire-rimmed glasses and dry them with his T-shirt. I wonder if he's Italian. Are Italians tall? Maybe he's on vacation here and—hmm. He reminds me of someone . . . I process the thought in my memory bank for a second . . . and then it pops up on my brain screen. Of course. He reminds me of Oliver Pollen, the swine. This boy is taller than Oliver. Of course. And darker. More Mediterranean. But he has that same swashbuckling walk, that aura of confidence, that self-possessed quality about him that Oliver had.

Oliver "Bad News" Pollen. It took weeks of talks last year with Martha to get him out of my system. I was such a wreck, I burned two pear tarts, accidentally squashed one perfectly wonderful angel's food cake, my key lime pie tasted like green beans, and I cooked a pot roast that was so hard to chew, I could have used it to re-sole my paratrooper boots.

Oliver had some nerve! All winter and spring we met twice a week to do chemistry homework, spent hours upon hours experimenting—and not just in the lab. Everywhere. On my bed. On his bed. Backstage, in school, in the green room, on a sofa during a tech rehearsal for a play he was working on. And then, come June, he walks off in the middle of the Museum of Modern Art with sex-bomb Roxanne Nielson on our end-of-the-year class excursion. One second we were stealing kisses under Matisse's *Dance*, and the next he and Roxanne were reported missing. How ironic! We had never even danced together! I never dance with *anyone*.

In the end, Martha and I concluded that Oliver was using me. He needed a strong lab partner so he wouldn't fail chemistry. Okay—he was a lousy bastard. But how does that make *me* feel?

The Italian boy has his glasses back on, and his eyes are scanning the car. The lenses are very thick, like the bottom of a Coke bottle, and his eyes are magnified. But he doesn't look nerdy or silly. The glasses give his buccaneer flair an intellectual edge.

I watch as the boy's eyes target into Carlotta. She notices him, sits up, uncrosses her patent-leather booted legs, and leans slightly toward him. Uh-oh. The slut's mating ritual. But he's looking at me again now. He picks up his shopping bag. He's going to sit down next to *me*, I think. He's standing just behind the man with the rosary beads to his right and the little boy with his notebook and fountain pen to his left. He's facing both me and Carlotta and our two empty seats, one next to Carlotta, one next to me. I watch him start toward me, but then Carlotta reaches up, pulls off her headphones, throws her head back, and tosses her long, permed Olivia Newton-John curls to and fro. That does it. The boy makes a sharp right and sits down next to Carlotta. She throws me a smug little smirk, then turns her attention over to her prey.

Something's brewing inside me. I think I'm . . . disappointed. Yes. And maybe . . . humiliated? But I'm also, I think, somehow relieved. If he had sat down next to me, I probably wouldn't have known what to do or say, anyway . . . And there's another feeling stuck inside me, drifting around my body's fifth dimension, trying to emerge. I wade through layers of emotion until I know what it is. I'm . . . angry. Yes. I'm pissed off at competitive little Carlotta!

Disappointment. Humiliation. Relief. Anger. That's a lot of emotion to have to deal with. I inhale and exhale a couple of times, and then look down at the map on my lap. I will concentrate on my mission. I will forget Carlotta and her Italian gigolo.

I find U-Bahnhof Schönhauser Allee on my Berlin map again, follow south along Schönhauser until I get to Stargarder Strasse, then—

The schoolboy across from me gasps, and I look up. The train's stopping. Zoologischer Garten. He hastily gathers his notebook and his fountain pen, throws them into his bag, and darts through the door. I steal a glance at Carlotta and the boy in the black leather jacket. I hear her say, "Like a virgin. Madonna."

The Italian boy says something, but I can't hear him. And I don't hear Carlotta now either. I hate them. Both of them. I know it shouldn't matter. I'm leaving town on Saturday. But still.

I pull myself away from my thoughts and look down at my map. Edda gave it to me after I got lost trying to find the movie theater where they were playing *When Harry Met Sally* in English. I'd already seen the movie five times in New York, so it wasn't a catastrophe that I missed the first fifteen minutes. But Edda was waiting for me and was worried. Thus, the map.

I like Edda and I'm glad she's our neighbor, glad Fritz and I decided to take a city apartment instead of the place the university offered us in Dahlem. We talk sometimes, Edda and I. It's easy with her. She listens. I listen. I open up. She takes me in. She and Bo remind me of Fritz and Leonora. Once, in September, I started to cry when I was sitting with them at their kitchen table. Fritz was working late in Dahlem, as usual, and Edda and Bo and I were playing a couple of rounds of skat. Fritz and Leonora taught me how to play when I was nine—just after Gwen moved out and went to Vermont for her master's in writing. So there I was playing skat with Edda and Bo, and all of a sudden there were blobs of tears all over my cards. I hadn't realized how much I missed my mother.

We're pulling out of S-Bahnhof Zoologischer Garten. Someone sits down next to me. And I look up. It's a little girl. Her mother is sitting across from her. I immediately can tell they are East Germans. It's funny, but you can recognize someone from the East a mile away. Their cars you know by the smell even before you see them. The exhaust is really acrid. And the people you identify by the clothes. The stone-washed jeans look is a sure giveaway. The ski jacket. The cheap moon boots they, especially the children, wear everywhere except to the moon. The women with fluffy, permed hair, short in front, long in the back, the men with the same haircut but porcupine-like in front. I call it the "Rod Stewart." And then there are the men with their humungous beards, as if they had fallen asleep for fifty years and never shaved. Bo Brody calls it the "Rip Van Winkle."

Bo, originally from Southern California, is a sound engineer who has worked with practically everybody who's a name in the music business today. He's a wonderful host. He and Edda are always inviting people over. A few weeks ago, they gave this really nice Rosh Hashanah dinner where their baby, Renée, cried all the way through. Generally speaking, Jewish holiday dinners make me blue. They remind me of Leonora. And I don't enjoy being reminded of her. That's why I've been putting off going to Prenzlauer Berg. It scares me. I'm anxious that a blob of emotion might, like yeast in a cake, rise and rise and then suffocate me, engulf me in the icky, sticky way feelings do. But I have to go today. It's my last chance. And Leonora would never forgive me if I didn't see where she was born. Despite all, I know she would have wanted me to go. So I must. Now. On Saturday I'll be back in New York, back in my old neighborhood, back with Martha and—

"Excuse me?"

We're at S-Bahnhof Tiergarten, and the mother sitting diagonally across from me is looking at me. "Would you mind terribly changing seats with my daughter?" she asks me. "She would like so much to look out the window."

The little girl to my left smiles up at me, her eyes wide and hopeful. I stand up and she happily slides over to the window. "I'll sit here," I say to the mother, gesturing to her seat.

I sit down in my new seat. Bad move. I'm riding backward now, facing Carlotta and her Italian gigolo in the black leather jacket, across the aisle, just a step or two from me. They're deep in conversation. Actually, it's mostly Carlotta doing the talking—even though I can't hear her. The boy turns his head a moment, and his silver loop catches the light from the window. He stretches out his long legs. His shopping bag is standing upright in the aisle beside him. I wonder what he has in there. It looks heavy. Maybe it's a chunk of the Wall he's bringing back to his home in Sicily. Bo chiseled away at the Wall the other day near Checkpoint Charlie and gave me a couple of pieces to take home for Gwen. Or maybe the boy has a mini-keg of real German ale in the bag. At that party I went to with Carlotta, they had one. Or maybe—

The Italian boy looks my way for a split second. Our eyes lock . . . but then he's back on track and giving Carlotta his full attention. I turn away. The German man in the skipper's cap to my left is still staring blankly out the window. I stare out the window too, but there's nothing to see from my angle. Just foliage spooling by.

I'm hungry. I fumble around in my handbag in search of some leftover candy, but only find some spearmint gum. I'll have to buy something in the Friedrichstrasse train station.

I return to my map, return to Greifenhagener Strasse. My mother's birth house. I remember her telling me there were two courtyards, one leading into the other. My grandparents' apartment was in the first courtyard. Leonora mentioned a tree in the middle and how it was surrounded by a garden plot with flowers that everyone in the building had planted. But there were chickens back there, too, in the second courtyard, and they pecked at the flowers. So one day everyone got together, the kids too, and built this little stone wall between the courtyards. It had a door so the neighbors could still get in and out and use their courtyards as a shortcut, but it kept the chickens out. And then my grandfather, Hans Ohrbach, built a bench, my mother said, and someone else got a hose and a sprinkler, and in the summer everyone cooled off back there, and the little kids, like my mother, pranced around under the sprinkler. She could see it all from her bedroom window, she said. On the second floor. Maybe I can go up and see. I wonder if the tree's still there. The garden plot. The stone wall.

Leonora was almost seven when they left in 1938. It was summer. Early morning. The Ohrbachs were gone before anyone realized it. Off to Bremerhaven. To their ship. To America. They moved to Chicago, where my mother learned English, became an American citizen, then a teenager, and later a teacher.

When Fritz was fourteen, a company of liberating American soldiers passed through town on their way to Thuringia.

The war was over. It was spring. The children ran to meet the GIs. One of them tousled Fritz's hair and gave him a piece of pink bubblegum. Fritz was immediately enamored with America. A dozen years later, he was in Chicago getting his Ph.D. In 1957 he was invited to his professor's daughter's wedding. Fritz, like all the guests, joined hands in a circle and danced to "Hava Nagila." He had never danced to "Hava Nagila" before and has only rarely since, but he never let go of his partner's hand after that night. Ever. It was Leonora. Leonora Sophia Ohrbach, my future mother.

And the rest is history.

I slip my map back into my pouch. Through the window to my right, where Carlotta and the woman in the camel's hair coat are sitting, I can look into the apartments in the buildings we pass.

Carlotta laughs. I can't hear what she's saying, but she points out my boots to the boy.

Why is she showing him my boots?

She whispers something in his ear and laughs again.

I flush. It radiates from the crown of my head, to my ears, down my neck, and across my chest. What is so funny about big feet? What is so hysterical about a tall girl? People are always asking me, "What does it feel like being so tall?" And all I can say is, "Small. I feel very, very small." Like now, with Carlotta pointing to my feet. I just want to disappear. Into a crack.

The train is pulling into Bahnhof Bellevue. Carlotta gets up. Thank God! She's getting off!

She's saying good-bye to the Italian boy. He also gets up now to say good-bye. She starts for the door and gives me one of her ugly, snotty sneers. It's the straw that breaks the giant's back. On an impulse, I stick out my foot. *Bam.* And Carlotta trips right over it. *Uff.*

Unfortunately, my foot causes more havoc than intended. Carlotta falls into the man with the rosary beads. She drops her purse and he drops his rosary beads. The Italian boy reaches out to grab Carlotta and stumbles over his shopping bag, which crashes down. Carlotta gets up, rubbing her knee. "You and your big feet!" she mutters through clenched teeth.

"I'm sorry." I am. I really am. I didn't want to hurt her.

Carlotta picks up her handbag and heads for the door. I'm not so sure she even realizes that I tripped her on purpose.

"Okay?" the boy asks her, opening the door for her.

Carlotta nods.

They whisper at the open door.

People are getting in and out of the train. Someone accidentally kicks the shopping bag. Another person almost trips over it. I grab it up—it's heavy!—and I want to set it upright just as I'm aware of a rush of neon pink passing the window outside. Carlotta. Finally! She's gone! I'm about to bring the shopping bag to the boy who's standing at the door, waving to Carlotta, but someone bangs into me. The carton slides out of the bag, crashes to the floor, bursts open, and out spill hundreds, literally hundreds, of Legos in all sizes, shapes, and colors—brown and red bricks, gray plates, heads without torsos, red-striped torsos without arms, a parakeet, a monkey, a sword, a treasure chest. The boy takes in the mess and blanches. If this were a movie, I'd call it *Curse of the Teenage Klutz*: "The awkward tale of an oafish girl and the boy who almost throttled her." Boy, oh boy, am I in trouble!

Three

Pirates of Berlin

Some of the Legos survive the crash and remain in the carton. Hundreds of them don't and have to be rescued, quickly, before the train stops again, piece by piece.

The little East German girl brings me a flag with a skull and crossbones. I'm beginning to understand that we're dealing with pirates.

I take off my coat. It's too bulky and hot, what with me crawling around on the floor. The boy and I work in silence. Both of us are on our hands and knees, hastily putting pieces back into the box. Our heads are almost touching. I can smell the rich, thick leather of his jacket. And now I smell *him*. Sweat mixed in with something else. It's a pleasant scent, but I can't place it.

The boy's looking at me. He really looks Italian up close.

"I'm . . . sorry," I stammer in English. "Really."

But he just returns to the task at hand. I can't read his face. Maybe he doesn't understand English?

The little girl is happy to be a part of the rescue team. She skips up and down the aisle asking people if they've seen pieces. Everyone's bending down and having a look. I am the cause of all this commotion. Talk about not wanting to attract attention!

By the time we roll into Lehrter Stadtbahnhof, the last stop in West Berlin, about two minutes later, the Legos are back where they belong. The boy puts the top on the box. There's a picture of a pirate ship on it with sails. "Black Seas Barracuda" is the name of the set. The price tag says DM 159. A small fortune!

"Here," I say to the boy, holding open the shopping bag for him so he can slip the carton in. At this close proximity, I catch that faint pleasant scent of his again. I don't think it's cologne. I breathe it in. And then I know what it is. It reminds me of a campfire. In the summer. Out in the country. No, not the campfire itself, but the surrounding trees. The *cedar* trees. That's it. Cedars. Delicious.

The little girl runs up to the boy and hands him a completed mini-figure: a pirate with a red-striped torso, blue hips and legs, and a sword in its hand. It has dark, curly hair, an eye patch, a stubbly chin. "*Hier!*" she says.

"*Danke*," says the boy, and slips the little pirate into his jacket pocket.

I look at him. "If any Legos . . . are lost, I . . ."

"Forget it!" he says, throwing himself back on his seat. He swats me away with a hand gesture. As if I were a pestering fly. At least that's what it feels like.

I'm embarrassed. I move away from the scene of my crime, one door down, look out the window with my back to the boy. I'm aware again of that chemical disinfectant smell. It's treacherous. Maybe I should take some back to New York with me and package it in spray cans. It can be used as a defense weapon for women when they jog after nightfall.

Outside, I see a high watchtower. We must have crossed into the East. And there's the Wall, zigzagging through an expanse of barren land and sand. And minefields? Another watchtower, not as high, spools by. The Reichstag looms in the distance, flat against a gray sky. I've never seen the Wall from this angle, from up here, hurtling toward and then past it. The snow flurries are gone. And we are now definitely in the East. We've stepped back forty years. I can see the back of the Reichstag and a hodgepodge of gray pockmarked buildings, some without windows like a skeleton's skull. It's a set for a film noir. Or for *The Spy Who Came in from the Cold*. Two men in trench coats are walking across what looks like a factory parking lot. Spies exchanging intelligence? Or just two factory administrators off to an early lunch?

Behind me, somewhere, is Signor Lego in his black leather jacket. Maybe he's going to East Berlin too. Or beyond. Leipzig. Dresden. Warsaw. Prague. Budapest. Or then again, maybe he's just switching to another West line. Maybe he's going north to Frohnau. On my U- and S-Bahn map, you can see that a bunch of train lines intersect at Friedrichstrasse.

My stomach growls.

The train screeches to a halt at Friedrichstrasse. Where do I go now? Fritz says I can't get lost, there are signs everywhere, or I should just go where everyone else is going. Okay. That's what I'll do.

At the other end of the platform, I see a bridge that expands across the station and men standing guard, overseeing the goings-on, walking nervously back and forth like lions in the gladiator's arena. Wow. Are they there to make sure East Germans don't try to escape over the tracks to the West? But the Wall's open now. They don't have to guard anymore. People can just walk over to the West, or take a train over or a car. So why are the guards still up there? Out of habit?

I pass an Intershop, and just behind it is a staircase with a sign to the border crossing point, GRENZÜBERGANGSSTELLE. I guess that's where I have to go, but I'm hungry, so I line up on the other side of the Intershop kiosk where the woman in the camel's hair coat is also standing. Out of the corner of my eye, I notice the boy in the black leather jacket whisk by. He must have been right behind me.

I'm aware of a slight vibration under my feet. That's strange. There's no train moving in or out of the station. To my immediate left, a monstrous steel wall rises from the last track to the ceiling. I wonder if there's something behind it. Or was the vibration *under* me? The subway?

"Next, please," the saleslady in the Intershop calls out.

The next customer, a man, points to a row of liquor bottles, but I can't hear what he says.

Once, when Carlotta Schmidt was still pretending to be my buddy, it must have been in early September, she, her older sister, Marita, and I took the U6 train to Friedrichsstrasse. They wanted to buy cigarettes in the subway station Intershop. They said it was much cheaper to buy them duty-free in an Intershop than in a normal store in West Berlin. Apparently lots of West Berliners do it, even though it's against the law to take the duty-free goods back into West Berlin—unless, of course, they were really visiting in the East. The whole idea seems very complicated, the Intershop being yet another East German anomaly that defies logic. Sometimes Fritz explains to me what he's currently working on. He talks about molecules, their life stages, their symmetry, their relationship to lasers and light and whatnot, and, frankly, theoretical chemistry sometimes make more sense to me than Intershops, stores that cater to foreigners with West currency, but not necessarily to East Germans. East Germans can go in, browse the shelves, and see what they'd love to have *if* they had West currency. But they rarely did. It seems so cruel—like the teachers who make little schoolkids write with a fountain pen.

In any case, Marita bought the cigarettes and then hid them in her bag. On the way back, until we switched to the U7, we felt like criminals and had to keep our eyes open for West Berlin customs police. Sometimes they frisked you on the train, looking for illegal cigarettes or liquor or perfume from—

"You better watch out," a voice says, startling me out of my thoughts. It's the woman in the camel's hair coat. "He's pretty tight." She points to a bearded man in jogging pants and a pea jacket walking toward us on the left.

When Carlotta, Marita, and I bought the cigarettes at the Intershop, there were weird-looking guys loitering there too. Apparently these Intershops are hang-outs for derelicts because the alcohol is cheaper here.

"He's plastered. He's going to fall off the platform," says the woman.

The man, wearing sneakers with the laces open and flopping around his ankles, is tiptoeing. He swerves to his left and shakes hands with a man in jeans, an army jacket, and a cast on his left foot. I assume that he's also drunk. He's leaning against the kiosk and watching the woman in the camel's hair coat. She's talking now to the saleslady behind the counter. "The large bottle," she says. "Chanel. The eau de toilette."

"Me, too!" the man in the foot cast slurs. "The large bottle. Eau de cognac."

The woman pays him no heed.

"I'll even take the small bottle!" calls out the drunk in jogging pants. "S'il vous plaît."

38

The men laugh raucously.

"Quiet!" shouts the saleslady behind the window.

The woman in the camel's hair coat pays for her perfume and turns to me. "They're trashed. Just ignore them."

"Thanks," I say as she leaves.

"What'll it be, young lady?" the saleslady asks impatiently.

I don't see any sandwiches or pretzels or franks. Nothing halfway substantial.

"Gotta mark?" the drunk with his foot in a cast asks me.

I shake my head, more out of caution than anything else.

"Hello?" says the saleslady, raising her voice over the din. "I'm talking to you."

She means me.

"Then how about *two* marks?" says the man, laughing at his own joke. His teeth are mossy-looking, as if fungus were growing on them.

"Get outta here!" the saleslady shouts at the two men.

They're hovering over me now. I'm aware of a strong, sour odor.

"That," I say to the saleslady pointing to a huge bar of half-bitter chocolate. It's so huge, I'm sure I'll still be working on it when I fly home.

I need to get away from these men and their foul smell. I pay the saleslady quickly and turn to the steps. But the men are following me. They reek of alcohol.

"Three marks?" asks the drunk with the foot cast.

"Four?" says the drunk in the jogging pants.

"Go away!" roars a voice in English.

The boy in the black leather jacket has appeared from nowhere. He swoops toward us, waving his arm as if he were brandishing a sword.

The men back off, shielding their faces.

The boy turns to me. "Okay?"

I just look at him.

"Follow me," he commands.

Do I have an alternative?

I don't. He grabs me by the arm and pulls me to the steps where the sign points the way to the crossing point.

He has a very strong grip.

Four

When Mick Met Molly

Thoroughly baffled by the boy's unexpected entrance, I let him guide me down a staircase, its walls lined with bright orange tiles. I squint. The sudden color after all the gray is a surprise.

We've entered a labyrinth. I lose my sense of direction. We go down steps. And then down some more. More people join us in the corridors. We turn right. Then left. I am dizzy from the endless twists and turns of this underground maze. But mostly from the smell of disinfectant, which is, I am sorry to say, worse here than in the train—it is trapped in the walls of the corridors, it seems.

Air. I need air. And I definitely don't need this boy dragging me around. I'm perfectly capable of taking care of myself.

"This way," he says, speaking English.

"Listen," I say. "Thanks, but I'm fine." I wriggle out of his grip, but he still walks beside me.

Another turn and we're standing in front of two open doors. One sign says "NO ENTRANCE" and the other "ENTRY GDR." Both in German.

"Your passport?" he says. "You might need it."

"Might?" I am surprised by his use of the subjunctive. We *are* crossing a border, aren't we? There *is* an Iron Curtain here, isn't there?

He laughs, and I see that his teeth are a little crooked. "The control is changing each day," he says. His English is a little off. But the accent sounds almost American.

An East German guard appears. He looks like he's directing traffic. The people ahead of us hold up their IDs for him to see as they pass. I fumble around in my pouch looking for mine, but before I can pull it out of my bag, he waves us through.

"It's as I say to you. They are different each day," the boy says, grinning.

He definitely knows his way around. Maybe he's one of those smugglers the newspaper said they're clamping down on. Maybe he's smuggling Legos into the East for the Italian Mafia. Maybe—

Oh. We have now entered a large hall with a dozen or so doors with narrow cubicles behind them. I can tell because most of the doors are open. Hordes of people in more or less orderly rows are lined up behind the doors.

Each door has an inscription above it: "DIPLOMATS," "CITIZENS BERLIN (WEST)," "CITIZENS BRD," "CITIZENS OTHER COUNTRIES," "CITIZENS GDR." I'm confused. Why aren't West Berliners considered West Germans? And why is West Germany a category unto itself and not just an "other country" like the Netherlands, for example?

The woman in the camel's hair coat, still reading her *Spiegel* magazine, is in the Berlin (West) line. In front of her, I see a splash of neon pink. No! It's Carlotta Schmidt! How'd she get here so fast? But then I look again and see it's someone much older, and she's not wearing a tube dress but a pink wool skirt.

The thin man with the skipper's cap and the briefcase slips by us and makes a beeline for the door marked "DIPLOMATS." Does this mean that he's not German?

But I'm right about the East German woman and her

daughter. At the far end of the hall, I watch them go through the door marked "CITIZENS GDR."

"There," says the boy, pointing to the "CITIZENS OF OTHER COUNTRIES" sign. "That is your line."

I can't seem to shake this kid off. What does he want from me? He's hovering around me like those two drunks. Although, I must admit, his cedar scent is far more pleasant.

We line up.

He puts his shopping bag down. He's looking at me, and I'm looking at him. What now? I suppose we'll have to start up a conversation.

"I'm sorry about the Legos," I say.

He shrugs. "I am sorry. It is my guilt. I should not have opened it."

It is my guilt. I almost giggle at his English. But I actually like the fact that he has apologized. Boys never do, even when they're in the wrong. Take Oliver "Bad News" Pollen as an example.

"I have played with them," he says. "This morning. The Legos. So it is my guilt. I forgive you. You were helping."

"*Grazie,*" I say, letting him know that I know he's not German but Italian.

His face lights up like a Christmas tree. He's not at all like Oliver Pollen, who always seemed to be concealing something.

"Ah!" he says. "You are Italian. I thought you were Swedish."

"Me? Italian? No, no. I thought *you* were Italian."

"Me?" he says.

I need to sort through this exchange. I buy some time by inching forward in the line. The boy inches forward too.

"Why did you think I was Swedish?" I say.

"Because of the height. The Swedish are so big."

Because of the height. I'll have to remember to write that one down. "But I'm not Swedish. Are you?"

"No. Why?"

"Because of the height."

I think he realizes I'm teasing him. His eyes, magnified out of proportion by his glasses, squint at me. His loop earring flickers, reflecting the light from the neon lamps above. "I am German," he says.

"You're *German?*" I answer in German, baffled.

"Yes—you speak German?" he says in German too.

"Yes!"

Now it's his turn to be surprised. "Are *you* German?"

"Yes! I mean no. Well . . . kind of. My parents are. I grew up in America."

We have forgotten all about speaking in English.

"America? Which America?" he asks.

His question takes me aback. "What do you mean 'which America'? America America."

"The United States of America?"

"Yes. Of course."

"Well, it could have been South America. Or Central America. Or Middle America."

This conversation is getting too geographical. And a little too personal. The boy's a total stranger. "Look, I—"

"Wow," says the boy. He looks like he just won the lottery. His eyes take me in. "A U.S. American."

"Excuse me?" says the man behind me. He points ahead of me. There's a gap between me and the woman in front of me. The boy picks up his bag, and we move forward.

"This isn't your line," I say. "Is it?" Maybe now, finally, I can get rid of him.

He smiles. "You're right. It's not."

He doesn't move.

"Well . . . it was nice meeting you," I say.

I can't give him a bigger hint. I turn my back to him and look down my line. There are four people in front of me.

The boy taps my shoulder. I turn back around. He holds out his hand. "Mick. As in Jagger."

It's funny the way Germans are always shaking hands. Even the kids. Once they stick out a hand like that, there's not much else to do but take it. So I take his. It's hot. Not sweaty. Just hot.

"Molly," I say. "As in Lenzfeld."

He releases my hand. "Jagger," he says. "is not really my name."

"Oh, really?" I say in mock astonishment.

"Maier. Michael Maier. But everyone calls me Mick."

He throws me a wink. And then, as if he just remembered something, he picks up his bag. "I better hurry," he says. He waves good-bye. "See you around, Molly as in Lenzfeld."

And he's gone. Just like that.

I watch him rush by the lines for West Berliners, then the line for West Germans, and finally line up at the far corner of the hall where the East German mother with her daughter had been standing.

That's interesting. He's from the East. An East German without a Rod Stewart or a Rip Van Winkle.

I watch his line weave its way toward its door, but then the man behind me leans over and asks me to *please* move forward. I do. And when I look back to catch another glimpse of the boy, he and his shopping bag have disappeared.

So that's that, I suppose. Good. Now I can concentrate on

my mission. He was distracting me. Besides, he wasn't even my type. We have nothing in common. Nothing except big feet, of course. I tear open my chocolate bar and break off a piece.

It's 11:49. I left the apartment over an hour ago. I'm next in line in the cubicle. I watch the East German border control officer in a gray uniform raise his arm, stamp something, and then hand the woman her passport back with a piece of paper sticking out of it. His movements are precise; he expends as little energy as possible. He turns to me and motions with a single hand movement that I should come forward. Fritz said that when he was here in August the doors were closed and they opened up automatically with a humming sound when it was your turn to enter—as if an invisible ghost had opened the gate leading down to the underworld.

The border official looks at my passport. Then at my face. Then at my passport again.

I look at the wart on his nose, then at the herpes on his upper lip, then at the wart again. It has three distinct hairs sprouting from its very center. I know it's impolite to stare, but there you go.

The border official has his eyes riveted to my passport. He asks me in English what kind of visa I need. "A nonstop transit visa," he says mechanically without looking up from my passport, "a transit visa with a seventy-two-hour stopover, a standard entry-and-exit visa, or a day visa?"

"I'll take one of each."

His head jerks up. He's not sure if I'm joking or not. A point for me.

Actually, I'm not sure what the difference is between a standard entry-and-exit visa and a day visa, but Fritz said to choose the day visa. So I do. "A day visa, thank you," I say with a smile.

"Five marks," the officer says, deadpan. He waits a second or two and then adds, "Please." The *please* has a serrated edge to it, more a command than a request.

I pay without any more jokes.

He writes. He stamps. He writes again.

I look around, discover a mirror above me. I look for a hidden camera. Or a hidden microphone. I find neither. Maybe I've seen too many spy movies, but it's hard not to feel a little anxious. I wonder if they have rooms tucked away for questioning, rooms with padded doors so you can't hear what's going on. Everyone these days is talking about the Ministry for State Security, the Stasi, its iron rule, its perniciousness. What if—

"Fraülein." The man gives me back my passport with my visa, a little stamp glued to it: "Administrative fee M 5."

I turn to the cubicle's exit door. It's open, but it hums anyway, signaling to me that I may now leave. Maybe the man forgot that the Wall is down and pressed the button out of habit.

Once outside, I follow the flow of tourists to the cashier, where I exchange the mandatory DM 25. Some kids in my class who've been to East Berlin say it's hard spending the 25 East German marks you get in exchange. There isn't very much to buy in East Berlin, they report, and everything is poorly made, anyway. Fritz says I should buy books. Edda says I should buy those sweet plastic egg cups that are shaped like chickens. Bo says I should buy sheet music. My girlfriend Martha Rosen wants Russian caviar. Our German teacher says we should buy a skipper's cap.

There's a bottleneck at the long counters used by customs for checking bags and suitcases, but the men here don't look as if their lives depended on being thorough. They wave me through like the customs officials at West Berlin's Tegel Airport. Nobody frisks me or stops me or questions me. I'm a free woman.

I pull open a heavy iron door, walk out of the border control center, and enter the station's waiting area. I'm still in the same Friedrichstrasse train station. I'm still in the same city. But—very weird—I'm actually in another country.

"Ahoy!" says a voice, startling me.

I whip around.

It's Mick as in Jagger.

"Welcome to the East," he says, grinning. "What took so long?"

Five

The Siberian Express

"So where are you off to?" Mick as in Jagger asks me. He's leaning against a railing, unflustered, untroubled, his arms folded, a head above the other people waiting for friends and family to emerge from border control. Was he actually *waiting* for me?

"I . . . I have to go somewhere," I say.

"Obviously." He straightens up to his full height. "And where exactly is 'somewhere'?"

I don't know what to say, so I pretend I haven't heard him and look past the crowd, hoping to find a sign for the S-Bahn to Alexanderplatz. I pick up that awful disinfectant smell. Here, too? Do they use the same product *everywhere*?

"I get it," he says. "You want me to *guess* where you're going. Right?"

Before I can say "wrong," he puts his hand on my shoulder. "We're in the way," he says, guiding me away from a wave of senior citizens now sweeping through the exit.

I'm distracted by the pressure of his hand on my shoulder. And by its warmth. We take a few steps, weaving through the crowd, and then he lets go. Strangely, I still feel the imprint of his hand.

We are in the middle of the station's concourse. There's an exit to our left leading to the street. It's cold here. And drafty. The walls are grimy and gray, the station uninviting. I look at my watch. It's 12:10. I'm on a mission. It's time to go.

"Okay, let me guess," he says. "Let me guess where you're going." He looks heavenward, feigning deep thought. "East?"

All right, I'll play his game for a moment or two. "If you come from the West, everything behind those doors is the East, isn't it?"

He rubs his stubbly chin, looks me up and down, from my bob to my boots. It's a little embarrassing standing there in a shearling duffle coat in the middle of a drafty train station with an East German boy appraising me. Embarrassing, yes, yet . . . intriguing.

"My gut instinct tells me," he says, "that you're about to hop on the Siberian Express to Novosibirsk. You definitely look like someone who's prepared for the taiga."

I giggle. "It's the boots. In fact, I think they were actually made there. Maybe I'll book Novosibirsk next summer, but today I'm sadly not traveling quite as far east."

"A little closer to home? Then how about . . . Minsk?"

Where exactly is Minsk? In Russia? Poland? Lithuania? Martha Rosen's grandparents were from Minsk. "More west," I say.

"West of Minsk? Let me think."

He's funny, this Mick. I can practically see a comic book bubble above his head while he ponders.

"How about the Pergamon Museum?" he says.

"Much warmer. But no."

"The top of the television tower?"

I roll my eyes.

"The French Dome? Palace of the Republic? The Soviet—"

"Prenzlauer Berg," I say. "The subway station Schönhauser Allee."

Mick seems genuinely surprised. "Really? Are you visiting someone?"

50

Isn't it enough that I told him where I'm going? Do I have to tell him the story of my life? Or my mother's? "I'm just looking at a building. Maybe an apartment," I tell him.

He looks interested. "You're looking for an apartment? I know a building on Stargarder Strasse. It has two empty apart—"

"No, no. I'm not looking for a place to rent."

"Rent? Who's talking about renting? Just take one. They're vacant. You can think about renting later."

"Just take one?" I say, incredulously. "How can you just take an apartment? You mean squat?"

He shrugs. "No. It's empty. The people left. Just take it and then go—"

"But I don't need an apartment!" I protest. Is that what kids do here when they want a place to sleep? They just go and take empty apartments?

"Sorry," he says a little defensively. "It was only a thought."

Did I just hurt his feelings? "Thanks, anyway, for the offer," I say kindly.

He gives me a half smile.

We shuffle our feet a moment or two. I think it's time to go.

"Do you live here?" the boy asks suddenly. "In Berlin?" He says it rushed, as if he's afraid he might lose courage and never have the chance to ask again.

"Yes," I say, because it seems easier just to say yes, be done with it, and go.

He's beaming. "Good. Good."

"Well, I have to get going."

"Sure." He picks up his bag. "I'll go with you."

He wants to go with me? But why? "No. Please. Don't. I'm perfectly—"

"I'm going that way, anyway. To Birkenwerder."

"Birkenwerder?"

"North. At Schönhauser Allee I switch to the S-Bahn to Oranienburg."

"But—"

He takes a step toward me, one menacing step. "Listen," he says. It's almost a whisper. "You're the first American I ever met in my life. You're the capitalists. The bad guys. They built this wall around us to keep you out. They called it 'an anti-fascist protective barrier.' You don't really think I'm going to let you get away so fast now. Do you?"

An anti-fascist protective barrier? Is *that* what they were told the Berlin Wall was? If so, it doesn't look like Mick quite swallowed it whole.

He takes another step toward me. His loop earring jiggles. And I can smell the cedar trees again. His eyes, magnified behind his wire-rims are huge pools, dark, deep.

"So?" he says. "What do you think?"

I have no idea what I think, because suddenly I feel a thud. In my chest. And then another one. It's very intense. And a little confusing. It must be the cedar. Or his eyes. Or that whispery, dark voice of his. Something about this boy is making my chest go *thud-thud-thud.* And the thuds are making it difficult to sort through what he just said. But his words are starting to make sense. I'm the forbidden stranger and therefore exotic. And actually, now that I think about it, I've never met an East German. Maybe I shouldn't let him get away so fast either.

"Okay," I say, sighing, as if it were the greatest of sacrifices. "Take me to your leader."

He nods, triumphant, then starts off toward a staircase with a big *S* for the S-Bahn. "The S-Bahn east," he says. "Off to Novosibirsk."

I gulp down some air. This is a big step. Even for a size-twelve shoe.

Mick and I are walking up the steps to the S-Bahn, side by side. Halfway up the staircase, he stops short.

"What?" I say, confused.

"How about something to eat first? There's a café a few blocks from here that—"

My first reaction is: no. Things are happening too fast. I get stuck when things change too rashly. I lock down. I was just getting used to the idea that we were going to have a little cultural exchange on the S-Bahn to Alexanderplatz and now, suddenly, he wants to eat something.

I shake my head. "I really don't have that much time."

I'm the turkey doctor for tonight's Thanksgiving dinner in case something goes wrong. I told Edda I'd be back at six. Which means I should be back here, at Friedrichstrasse, by—

"No time for a snack?" he says.

"I have to be back for dinner and—"

"That's not for hours!"

He's breaking down my resistance. Well . . . I suppose I have enough time. And I *am* hungry. "Isn't there a place to eat here?" I ask. "In the station? So we don't lose time?"

"Lose time?" Mick grins. "The second you came through that iron door downstairs," he says, "you didn't just change countries. You changed time zones too. The clocks run different here. They're slower. You learn to be patient in the East."

I just stare at him. Am I going to be sorry I agreed to this?

Mick stares back, shrugs, then turns around and gestures to a dark corner of the station. "I suppose we could go to the Mitropa."

Mitropa? It doesn't sound like the Ritz, but it's just a few steps away. I wonder if it will smell of disinfectant in there too.

"Hey," I say, as we start walking to the restaurant. "I have a question for you."

"Shoot."

"What's this smell?" My arm sweeps through the station.

"What smell?"

"This antiseptic smell. It's sharp. And kind of stale. It's everywhere."

Mick sniffs the air. Then looks at me. Sniffs again. He shakes his head. "Sorry," he says. "I don't smell anything."

Six

Mitropa, Mon Amour

The Mitropa Restaurant has the charm of a makeshift Salvation Army soup kitchen: poor lighting, mismatched tables and chairs, grimy walls, air so thick with smoke you can practically eat it with a spoon like gruel. And it may be the only place in East Germany that doesn't smell of disinfectant. It smells like cabbage. It is all-consuming. It clings to the walls, the floor, the plates, the waitresses' uniforms—*everything* here reeks of cabbage in its manifold variations: plain boiled cabbage and fancy red kraut, cauliflower and sauerkraut, brussels sprouts and stuffed cabbage leaves.

The restaurant is crowded. A waitress with a dough-like complexion marches up to us. The name badge pinned to her white top is on upside down, but I have no trouble seeing that she's "COLLEAGUE URSULA FELSBURG."

"How many?" she barks at us.

"Just the two of us," says Mick.

"Stay here! You will be seated!" she says, and then storms away.

I look at Mick. "The friendly type."

"I bet she suspects she's losing her job. Now that everyone's talking about reunification, she's worried that her days are probably numbered." He leans forward and whispers in my ear. "Stasi."

"She's a *spy*?" I say, utterly surprised.

"Shh. If they know we're talking about them, they'll never seat us."

I lower my voice. "But how do you know she's a spy?"

"It's an open secret. They're all spies. Or at least most of them. You *had* to be to work at this restaurant. Because of the border. The people from the West. The West currency. It's the ideal place to collect and pass information. Some of the customers too."

"Are you sure?"

I look at three men in droopy suits drinking beer at a table to the right of us. They're all wearing sideburns and mustaches and speaking a language I do not understand. Maybe they're Czech. Or Ukrainian. Perhaps Hungarian. I'm not an expert. "Them?" I mouth soundlessly at Mick.

Mick shakes his head. "Harmless. Cardiologists from Leningrad. They're here for a conference. I overheard them speaking Russian."

"You speak Russian?"

"It's compulsory. In school."

"Let me hear you say something."

"What?"

"Anything. Something you learned."

Mick says something in Russian. It sounds pretty good to me. "And?" I ask. "What did you say?"

"I said, 'Honorable comrade, best wishes on the occasion of International Woman's Day.'"

This guy's a riot!

"And you can really understand those men?" I want to know, gesturing toward the table with the three Russians.

"I understood the word 'conference,' and they look like doctors, don't you think?"

56

Is he joking or not? I'm not quite sure. "And English?" I ask. "You learned your English in school too? Your accent sounds American. It's very good."

"Really?" he says. "What a compliment. Thanks. I like to think I'm good with accents. I learned it in school, but most of my English comes from rock music. From lyrics. We heard West radio. All the time. We weren't really supposed to, but we all did it."

I have a vision of the boy locking himself in the coat closet, his long body crouched over with a transistor radio to his ear.

In the middle of the room, I notice two couples at a table paying for their meal. Will we be seated there? A waiter is clearing away their dishes. Mounds of purple remain on the plates.

"Where exactly are you from in . . . America?" Mick asks. He emphasizes the word *America*, poking fun at my previous faux pas.

"New York."

His eyes go round with wonder. "Really? Wow. And what are you doing here?"

"My father's here on a research grant. For a year. At the Free University."

"No kidding?"

Mick may have cultivated a tough outer shell, but inside he's like a little kid in a toy shop, *ooh*ing and *aah*ing at every turn. I wish I had his exuberance. But it's hard when you have a touchy nose like I do and the waiter is whisking by with huge mounds of leftover red cabbage. The sight of it may actually cause me to spit up the chocolate I ate.

"What's this doing here?" says a voice.

We whip around and see that Colleague Felsburg has suddenly appeared again. She's pointing to Mick's shopping bag, which is standing upright a bit to the left of us. "Take it out of the aisle, please!" she commands.

The waitress, her hair dyed so black it glows blue, is very bossy for one so young. She's maybe thirty, certainly not older than my sister, Gwen. I can't imagine Gwen talking to her customers at that Mexican restaurant in Vermont like that. They'd burn her at the stake like a witch in old New England.

"Immediately!" Colleague Felsburg says, giving the bag a teensy kick. "It's a safety hazard!"

Mick obediently wedges the bag between his long legs, and she huffs and puffs away. "It's better to keep out of the way of sensitive waitresses," he says, giving me a wink.

"As sensitive as a toilet seat."

We giggle. It's a nice moment. I feel like I may yet have a sense of humor.

"What's he researching?" Mick asks after a moment. "Your father."

"He's a theoretical chemist," I say. "But, please, don't ask me what a theoretical chemist is. You don't want to know. It's very complicated."

Mick's eyes narrow, but he says, "Okay. Change of subject. So why aren't you in school today? You *are* a student, aren't you?"

"No. I'm a 132-year-old vampire spy from Transylvania. It's Thanksgiving. My school's off. It's the American school."

"Ah."

"*Erntedankfest,*" I say, translating for him.

"I know what Thanksgiving is," he says, a bit defensively. "I saw that Woody Allen movie. *Hannah and Her Sisters.* They celebrate Thanksgiving like ten times."

"Really? That movie was in East Berlin?"

"You'd be surprised at how many things slip through that anti-fascist protective barrier. So, yes, I know what Thanksgiving is. I just didn't know Thanksgiving was *today*. Is that why you have to rush home?"

Mick's a good listener. That's more than I can say for Oliver "Bad News" Pollen.

"I said I'd be home by six," I say. "We're cooking a turkey. And I have to do the stuffing. And I also have to—"

For a moment an image of Carlotta Schmidt flashes in front of me. A splash of pink neon, a flurry of blond permed curls, a sneer. I wonder what she'd think if she saw me with Mick? Maybe I'll tell her tonight I spent time with him and then watch her blanch.

"And?" he says.

"And what?" I say, startled.

"You started to say, 'And I also have to—'"

"Oh, right. I also have to do the dessert."

"Which is?"

"A walnut cake. I call it the Berlin Wall-Nut Torte."

He groans at my silly joke. "I'd like to try it one day."

"At your own risk. It has a disinfectant frosting." Boy, oh boy, am I on a roll or what?

The two couples that just paid are walking toward the exit now. The waiter whips their red cabbage-stained tablecloth off the table, turns it around to the other side, and puts it back on.

"And you?" I ask Mick. "Why aren't *you* in school?"

"I graduated. I did my exams last summer."

"Good for you."

"And now I'm studying acting." This he says proudly.

Yes. I can easily picture him rooming with Ethan Hawke in *The Dead Poets Society*. Or going back to the future with Doc Brown. Or he could star in his own movie: *Life in the Gray Zone: See! Clothes and hairstyles that should have been outlawed years ago! Hear! Hours of secret audio surveillance! Taste! Just how awful cabbage can be!*

I look at him, his unshaven face, the curly, messy black hair, his huge dark eyes. His lanky self-assurance. "Acting suits you," I say.

Our eyes lock. And I get that thud thing going again in my chest. What *is* it? Excitement? Attraction? Pleasure? Curiosity? Fear? All? None?

This time Mick is the first to look away. He shifts his weight from one hip to the other. He sticks his thumbs in his jeans pocket, his eyes wander through the restaurant. He's trying not to look at me. What's wrong? What did I do now?

"What?" I say.

Mick clears his throat. "You're the first person I ever met who didn't ask me why I'm not in the People's Army."

"The People's Army?"

"Military service always comes right after graduation," he says.

My stomach growls, but if Mick hears, he doesn't let on. I feel queasy. And my coat is getting heavy and hot. I search around in my pouch for my gum. Maybe it'll settle my stomach until I get used to the cabbage smell. Or until I get something to eat.

"'GDR for Beginners,'" I quip. "Thanks for the army data." I offer Mick a piece of gum. He takes it. Sniffs it. Opens it up. Pops it in his mouth.

I see that our table is almost ready. The waiter has just returned with a salt-and-pepper shaker set.

"So why aren't you in the army?" I ask, taking a strip of gum too.

"Sadly I was rejected."

"Sadly? Ha-ha. And why? Flat feet?"

He ignores the question.

I look at his glasses. "Are you legally blind?"

"It's a long story."

"And the short version?"

"I was lucky. I always am. It's a mystery. No one thought I'd get accepted to acting school either. Least of all me. Before I auditioned, they said I was absolutely too tall to be an actor. If you're short they can put you in elevated shoes, but giants cause problems."

Giants cause problems. Tell me about it. It's the story of my life. But clearly it's not the story of *his.* "They took you, anyway," I say.

"They did! That's what I'm saying! All six feet four inches of me! It's a mystery!"

His sentences all end with exclamation points. Mine trail off in ellipses. We're so unalike. Yet . . . our eyes meet again . . . I must admit, it's nice locking eyes with someone who's actually taller than me, whose dark eyes I can look up into, magnified a thousand times. My heart does a quick somersault. And then another one. And then it decides to do a couple of cartwheels and—

"The blood- and liverwurst platters!" barks Colleague Felsburg to my right, at the cardiologists' table, interrupting my thoughts, my cartwheels, everything. Damn her. I watch her plonk down three steaming plates with heaps of potatoes, mounds of sauerkraut, a thick blob of mustard, and two fat sausages each—one red, one brownish, their slippery skins slimy with grease. I am surprised that I have not become a vegetarian in Germany. And I am more surprised that my mouth waters at the sight of the sausage. The taste for it has been programmed into my German marrow, I suppose, by my German mother and my—

"We're ready to seat you!" says the waiter now. His badge, I see, reads "COLLEAGUE GOETZ STEINMETZ."

Strangely enough, the two seats Colleague Steinmetz offers us are neither at the recently vacated table nor together. One is at a table in the back where an elderly couple with a man, maybe their son, is sitting. The other seat is at the table with the cardiologists, where the smell of their steaming sauerkraut has begun to make its way to my poor nostrils.

Mick doesn't seem at all surprised that we've been offered seats miles apart from one another, but to his credit he refuses them. "We'd like to sit together," he patiently tells the man. "At that table." He points to the four recently vacated seats.

If looks could kill, Colleague Goetz Steinmetz is about to send us off to the kitchen and dunk us in the pot with the sauerkraut. Just the thought of it makes me feel sick. I bite down on my gum and pull up the collar of my flannel shirt. I breathe in the sweet laundry detergent scent.

"That is a table for *four!*" Colleague Steinmetz says, as if it were a capital offense in this country for two people to sit at a table set for three or more.

"But there's no one here waiting for the table," Mick points out. "Just us."

"Those are the rules!" says Colleague Steinmetz. "If you like, you can wait for a table for two."

Colleague Felsburg is now marching toward us. I have a premonition that she's coming to get me. She will drag me over to the table with the cardiologists and force me to sit down with them.

She walks right up to me. Under the light, I see that her frosty blue eye shadow phosphoresces. If I were a spy, I wouldn't wear fancy eye shadow. And I wouldn't dye my hair either. I'd dress and groom myself as low-key as possible. But then again, maybe she's not a spy.

Colleague Ursula Felsburg sticks her face in my mine. I flinch. Ready to battle. "You look sick," she says. "Let me get you a chair."

My mouth drops open. Before I can close it, she appears again with a chair and pushes me down into it. "It's the cabbage, isn't it?" she whispers in my ear. "It gets to me too. I have some antacid tablets in my handbag. Let me get one for you."

I am too surprised even to thank her.

"Do you want the seats I offered you or not?" says the waiter to Mick.

"Relax, Goetz!" says Colleague Felsburg to Colleague Steinmetz. "And give them that table for four!" And she's off.

But the smell of the sauerkraut from the cardiologist's table has become unbearable.

"Mick," I say. "I feel a little sick."

"You need some air. Let's just go."

I stand up, Mick takes my elbow with one hand—he really *does* have a strong grip—and with the other hand he snatches up his Lego bag, which, sadly, swings off to the side and slams right into Colleague Steinmetz.

"Are you out of your mind?" the waiter snarls, rubbing his shin.

"I'm sorry," Mick says. "Really. I didn't mean to."

We turn to go.

"You're leaving?" says the man, incredulous.

"We changed our mind," Mick tells him.

"If you want fast food," the man says, "go back to the West where you come from!"

As we start for the door, I see Colleague Felsburg return with a glass of water. "What happened?" I hear her say to Colleague Steinmetz.

"West kids!" says the waiter. And then with a scolding voice, he adds, "Uschi, your badge is upside down again. For Christ's sake! What will the guests think?"

But by then we're already out the door.

Seven

Mick in Legoland

We're back in the train station's drafty concourse. I shiver, but not because of the chilly air. There was something about that restaurant and the personnel that was so discouraging. But Mick, walking beside me, is different than them. I look at him with that pirate's loop in his ear, with his swashbuckling stride, his open face. He's so bold, so optimistic. A romantic.

"Some fresh air coming up," he says.

"It was the sauerkraut," I say. "Sauerkraut has always been my nemesis."

"You use big words," he says.

"You're a big boy."

I know I'm blushing. I can't believe I said that. *You're a big boy.* Is this what they call flirting? Is that what I'm doing here?

Mick guides me to the exit with his hand on my elbow. I can actually feel its warmth through the thick layers of my shearling coat.

A tall woman with silver hair passes by, and for a brief moment I see Leonora, my mother. I wonder if she was ever in this station as a little girl. Maybe she walked through this very exit that Mick and I are now passing through. I wonder what she would have thought of Mick. She'd probably say something like, "A strapping young man." She liked using words like that. *Nemesis. Strapping. Young man.*

"Friedrichstrasse," says Mick, taking his hand from my elbow. He points right and left. Friedrichstrasse is a busy street with lots of pedestrians, traffic, and those tiny little cars. We're standing under the tracks that cross through the street. Everything is loud under here. And dark. And smelly. Especially the exhaust fumes from the cars. There's a bookstore to the right of us, and across the street from us is another entrance to the train station, but a bus comes by, extra-long and serpent-like, like a Slinky—now that's something they don't have in West Berlin—and blocks the entrance from view.

We lean back against the wall and watch the people pass by. Mick laughs to himself and mumbles something, but I can't hear him because a train is passing above.

"What?" I say.

"This is a weapon!" He picks up his bag and shakes it. "Did you see that waiter's face when I accidentally banged into him?"

We both laugh. Colleague Steinmetz is definitely not on our team.

"Are they yours?" I ask. "The Legos?"

"Nah. For a neighbor. Viktor. My friend David's younger brother. He's ten. He saw them last weekend at KaDeWe when he was visiting West Berlin and wouldn't stop talking about them. So he decided to get them with his welcome money. I picked them up for him. You know what welcome money is, don't you?"

I nodded. You couldn't live in West Berlin and not know what it was. You couldn't miss the East Germans waiting in line in front of the banks to get their one hundred marks, a gift from the West German government for each visitor from East Germany. "But," I say, "I thought welcome money was only one hundred marks. The price tag on the box said one hundred fifty-nine."

"You should be a detective," he says, blushing. "The truth is, David and I agreed to chip in the rest if Viktor lets us play with the set whenever we wanted to. What can I say? I always wanted Legos."

Another Slinky bus passes by. I wonder why they don't have double-deckers like they do in West Berlin.

"When I was a kid," Mick says, "this boy on our block, Thomas, his grandmother lived in Hamburg, and she was always sending him packages filled with treats. Ritter chocolate. Haribo candy. Nutella. Canned pineapple." He points to his mouth. "Spearmint gum. And Legos."

"You don't have any of that here?"

"East brands. But it's not the same. West gum, West chocolate, West gummi bears, West everything was better. *Is* better. And the Legos—unbelievable! Thomas got them for his birthday. For Christmas. For good report cards. For bad report cards. For everything. The problem was, he never let us play with them. We were only allowed to *look* at them. He had this outer space collection with a space command center, a planet scooter, a moon taxi, a rocket landing runway, astronauts—mind you, not cosmonauts, *astronauts*. And it was set up like an altar on top of his dresser."

"So you don't have Legos in East Germany?"

"Something similar. Pebe. But it's not the same. Not as elaborate. You know, we didn't have any relatives in the West, so no one sent us West packages. But I didn't really mind. I didn't care about the sweets that much. But Legos! Now, that would have been a dream come true! So when Viktor saw the pirate ship, I could really empathize."

Empathy. It's another word my mother would have used. Understanding other people. Sharing their feelings. Do I do that? Do I feel their feelings? Do I even feel *mine?* But whatever empathy is, Mick has it, I'm sure.

"I think you'll be a good actor," I say.

"Yeah?" he mumbles. "Why do you say that?"

"Empathy."

"Well, thanks. Maybe." A train passes by, and he looks up. The sky is a gray-blue, and he squints at a cloud where the sun is trying to break through. "I should be in school now. This is the first time I've ever cut classes."

"Why didn't you go?"

Mick runs his fingers through his hair. "I got a late start this morning. It's a long story. Some other time."

Some. Other. Time. Does he really think there is going to be *some other time?* Maybe I should let him know that there won't be. Maybe I should let him know that in two days we'll be 4,000 miles apart and—

My stomach growls, and Mick hears it. He giggles and stands up straight. His leather jacket squeaks a little when he moves. "I think you need something to eat," he says.

"And I think you need to oil your jacket."

"Your coat doesn't squeak?"

"Not that I know of."

Mick puts his hand on my shoulder. Under my hood. As if he were going to pull me toward him. But he doesn't. Instead, his fingers slowly graze the surface of my coat. From the back of my neck, across my shoulder, to just below my collarbone. I have stopped breathing. It's the sexiest thing anyone has ever done to me. It's even sexier than sex itself. Definitely sexier than sex with Oliver Pollen.

"It's soft," Mick says.

"Yeah," I say.

68

"I've never felt anything this soft."

"Neither have I."

I can barely hear us over the din of the traffic now. Or is it the din of my heartbeat?

"You're right," he says. "It doesn't squeak."

His hand is resting on my chest. I want to close my eyes and luxuriate in the touch.

"Ouch!" I cry out.

Someone has banged right into me. An elbow jabs me in the side.

"Oh, I'm sorry!" says a heavyset woman trailing a shopping cart behind her. "But you're standing right at the exit." She walks past us, and her cart rolls over Mick's right boot.

"Ouch," he says, and we burst out in laughter.

I laugh so hard, I almost pee in my pants. Very embarrassing. But it's a wake-up call. I look at my watch. It's past 12:30. "Maybe we should get going," I say. "Is there a bathroom around here somewhere?"

Eight

Margot and Erich

I smell the toilets before I discover the sign announcing their presence. The disinfectant stench seems strongest here, mixed with the nasty odors associated with all public toilets. The thought of going down the dark steps into the train station's cavernous basement is not pleasant, but nature calls . . .

"Be right back," I tell Mick.

And he nods.

Women are lined up at the entrance to the ladies' room. A lavatory attendant stands sentinel at the door like a watchdog guarding a junkyard. She wears a blue smock over a red polyester flowered top, a dark skirt, and on her feet are sensible shoes that look the same all over the world: comfy and ugly. She is also wearing a wig that even a child would immediately recognize, especially since she is certainly beyond sixty and couldn't possibly have lustrous blond hair that shines like Barbie's, that is coiffed so perfectly and has slipped off center and is in danger of falling into the garbage pail beside her. I wonder if the woman bought this in the West with her welcome money.

A man in work clothes is standing on a chair scrubbing graffiti from the walls. Someone crossed out the words *Damen* and *Herren* and wrote *Margot* and *Erich*. *Very funny*, I think, as I search my bag for coins. *That's Margot, East Germany's*

First Lady, and her husband, Erich Honecker, the head of state.
The lavatory attendant wants 50 East pfennigs, but I don't
have East change. When I exchanged my 25 West marks, I
received two small bills that looked more like they were from
a game of Monopoly than real currency, a green bill worth 20
East marks and a purple bill worth 5. I find my wallet and
give the lavatory attendant 50 West pfennigs. In return she
gives me three pieces of toilet paper instead of two. I wonder
why they don't just put the roll in the stalls instead of tearing
sections off, piece by piece, and distributing them. Are they
afraid we will use too much paper? Who would even think
it? It is so rough, I could probably file my nails with it. Is this
what our social studies teacher meant the other day by East
Germany's "economy of scarcity"?

Afterward, I wash my face and hands and need to get a
paper towel from the attendant. Neatly arranged on her table are several packs of cigarettes, both East and West German brands, as well as an assortment of sweets and hygienic
goods—also from both Germanys, including sanitary pads,
tampons, emery boards, safety pins, tissues. And condoms.
Here is a woman clearly prepared for reunification.

When I come upstairs, Mick is gone. Maybe he went downstairs to Erich? I wait a few minutes. But he doesn't come.
He must be here somewhere! But where? Did he bump into
someone he knows? Is he browsing at a newsstand? I start
looking around, maneuvering among the crowds streaming
in and out of the station, looking for him, past East Germans, West Germans, West Berliners, foreigners, diplomats.
I brush shoulders with Stasi spies, senior citizens, border
officials, students. I steer past waiters and waitresses, CIA

agents who have come in from the cold. But Mick is nowhere. He's gone.

Gone? Is it possible?

I return to the stairs that lead down to the restrooms. He's not here.

And then it sinks in. He is truly gone.

I knew this would happen. I knew it. It always does. Because I'm awkward. And dull. And stuck, stuck, stuck. Who would want to spend time with me, anyway?

Mick is gone. Disappointment, hard and cruel, oozes through me. It's dead weight, heavy, like liquid lead, pulling me down, down, down. A horrible sense of abandonment overcomes me. I think I may cry. I *am* crying. I need air.

I exit to the left, a different exit than before, and lean against the outside wall. It's cold out here now without Mick. I inhale long breaths through my nose and exhale through my mouth. After Leonora died, Gwen wanted to get me interested in yoga. So I would relax. The only thing that helped, though, was the breathing. In through the nose. Out through the mouth.

The sun is shining somewhere above and behind me. I'm facing north, standing opposite a long line of people waiting for taxis. Every now and then, one pulls up. Across from me, I see a building with people lining up. I recognize it from a photograph Fritz showed me. "The Palace of Tears," he said. "That's where you go when you return to West Berlin. The departure checkpoint."

Maybe I should go back to West Berlin *now*. All I have to do is walk a few steps northwest, slip back into my crack, and everything will be forgotten and—

But I'm on a mission! It's my last chance. Why should I let some East German acting student change my plans? Leonora would never forgive me if I didn't go. Oh, what am I talking about? *I* would never forgive myself if I didn't go. It's something I *need* to do. No matter how hard.

I turn around and walk back into the station, heading for the S-Bahn sign. And just as I approach the stairs, I notice to the left of me a dark, towering shape swooping through the hall. It's Mick! He's running toward me. His shopping bag, in his left hand, is banging against his thigh. He's holding something in his right hand, but I can't quite tell what it is from this distance.

"Ahoy," he says when he gets to me.

He's out of breath. His cheeks are flushed. His eyes are ablaze. He was rushing. Was he rushing to get back to me? To me, Molly Beth Lenzfeld?

My disappointment has vanished. I am now feeling something entirely different, something I have never felt before, something light and giddy. It's as if my body were being pumped with helium. All the empty spaces in me are filling out with this . . . this feeling. But what is it? Joy? Whatever it is, I feel it in my toes. My chest expands. My pinkies tingle with delight. My ears itch with expectation. I want to float above the concourse and into the daylight.

"Sorry," Mick says, putting down the bag. "I had to go down the block for this. And there was a long line. And— well, here."

In each hand Mick is now holding what looks like a perfect oblong roll with a hole on top. It must have been skewered, because a frankfurter, doused in red sauce, fits right into it, its head sticking out of the top like a pig in a blanket.

"An East German specialty," Mick says, grinning like a little boy. "A *Ketwurst*."

Nine

The Iron Curtain

We're sitting in front of the Iron Curtain. It's made of steel. And it's very real, not just an idea, a concept, or an intellectual border between East and West like we learned in school. I could touch it if I were tiptoeing across the tracks like the mouse I spot down there now.

"Look!" I say, and give Mick a jab with my elbow. "A mouse."

It's hard to believe that the East German government actually erected an iron curtain *in the middle of a train station.* It seems almost more perverse than the Berlin Wall itself. There's the south side of the Friedrichstrasse station I came in on over an hour ago, and there's this side, the north side, where the East Berlin S-Bahn begins and ends. It's where East Berliners have sat for years waiting for their train home from school or work or shopping, where they could actually hear the announcements of trains arriving from and leaving to West Berlin. I'm astounded by the overwhelming physical presence of a complete lack of freedom.

"How could you stand it? How could you live with this . . . this—" I can't think of the proper word to describe this . . . this . . . "Monstrosity," I say.

"I was never here," Mick says. "I never had to look at it. Well, once. When I was little. But I don't remember anything in detail. I was with my mother. She'd met someone at work. Bjørn. A Swede who was here for a couple of weeks working on some project. And we brought him to the station to catch the train back to Stockholm. We all said good-bye at the departure building, and then my mother and I sat up here, right here, where we're sitting now, and for a very long time we listened to the trains going by on the other side. We could hear them come and go. And I remember my mother said, 'That's it. His train. The train to Sassnitz. To Sweden.'"

I take a bite of my *Ketwurst*. The sauce is watery and the frank itself is cold and spongy. But it's food. At least I hope it is.

A train from Alexanderplatz is arriving now right in front of us, concealing part of the Iron Curtain. Passengers climb out, whisk past us.

"Friedrichstrasse," announces a voice over the loudspeaker. "Last stop. The incoming train returns to Strausberg Nord via Alexanderplatz, Central Station, Ostkreuz, and Lichtenberg."

Directly behind us, on the most northern track of the station, people are getting into the train to Königs Wusterhausen via Alexanderplatz. It's next to leave. But we're not in a hurry.

"Hey!" Mick points to some red sauce that has dripped down my roll and landed on my boot. Good—the less sauce for me to slurp, the better.

"Do you know where the name *Ketwurst* comes from?" Mick asks.

"I bet you're going to tell me."

"*Ket*chup and wurst. *Ketwurst*."

"Ah!" I say, and pop the rest of the sausage in my mouth. I search my pockets for a tissue and find the train tickets that Mick validated for us instead. Funny: the tickets feel like they're made out of the same paper as the toilet paper downstairs, only *softer*. What irony.

I find a tissue and wipe my fingers off. "Dessert?" I ask, my hand diving into my pouch. It surfaces with the chocolate bar. Mick breaks off some chocolate. The train to Königs Wusterhausen is about leave.

"We'll take the next one," Mick says, chomping down on the chocolate. He savors the taste a moment.

"What does your mother actually do?" I ask as the train leaves.

"She's an artificial insemination technician."

I search his face to see if he's joking. I think not. I say the word—*Besamungstechnikerin*—out loud, trying to figure out what it is. "It sounds like something people only whisper about behind closed doors."

"For cows, Molly. For cows. Not people."

Molly. He said my name. I feel a rush of warmth gush through me, like that time when I was fourteen and I drank a shot of whiskey at Gwen's best friend's wedding. Molly. It sounds so nice coming from him. He even pronounces it like Americans do, with a drawn-out "a" instead of a short "o." Maa-li. Emphasis on the first syllable.

"It may not sound like it," Mick says, "but artificial insemination technicians are important people in the 'Workers' and Farmers' State.' The milk and cattle production in three co-ops are absolutely dependent on my mother's syringe."

He says it with such child-like earnestness, I have to laugh. "I bet you're going to be a comedian when you grow up," I say.

"My mother wants me to be an artificial insemination technician."

"You're joking!"

"Yes. Actually, I am."

I sock him in his arm. And we lean back and look at the train in front of us.

76

"Is this the next train out?" I ask Mick.

He nods.

I know we should get up and go in the train. I need to get to Prenzlauer Berg. He needs to get to Birkenwerder. But I'm having fun. Oliver Pollen and I never just hung out and talked. We were either studying chemistry or studying the Kama Sutra. We rarely had fun—aside from the sex, of course. But even that was kind of hello/good-bye, cut-and-dried, am I doing it right? Obviously, I wasn't. He left me for that Roxanne.

I hear a West train leaving the station behind the Iron Curtain. I think about Mick and his mother sitting here and waiting for the train to Sweden to depart. I turn to him. "Was your mother in love with that man?"

"Maybe," he says, as if a second before I mention it, he has thought about it himself too. "She never *told* me she was, but probably."

"And your father?"

Mick shrugs. "I never met him."

"Really?"

"Yeah. He was never part of the picture. They met when they were in training to become insemination technicians. And then it was over. We live with my grandparents."

Besamungstechnikerin, I say aloud. "It's a good word. You know what I like about German? The way you can build new words using smaller ones. German has all these compound words. It's like taking different colored Lego bricks that have nothing at all to do with one another and making something new out of them. *Besamung.* And *Techniker. Zeit* and *Geist* make *Zeitgeist. Blitz* and *Krieg* make *Blitzkrieg. Welt* and *Schmerz* make *Weltschmerz.*"

Mick is staring at me as if I were crazy.

"What? What did I say? What's wrong?" I ask.

"Nothing! Why do you always think something's wrong? It was a nice comparison. And I like your accent."

I'm instantly relieved. I lean back again against the bench.

Behind us another train has come in, spilling out passengers.

Mick makes himself comfortable and chomps down on a piece of chocolate.

"How about *Vergangenheit* and *Bewältigung*?" I say. "Take the noun *past*, add the noun *overcoming*, and it equals everybody's favorite *Vergangenheitsbewältigung*. What do you think of that word?"

"*Vergangenheitsbewältigung*," he says, thinking the word through, as if he were trying it on for size. "I never heard that one."

He's joking. He has to be. If there's one thing Germans have heard about, day in, day out, these past forty years since World War Two, it's got to be this: *Vergangenheitsbewältigung*, coming to terms with the past. Or was it just *West* Germans who struggled through the muck and mire of their past?

"Did you just make it up?" Mick wants to know. He tickles me in my side. "You did, didn't you?"

"No way!" I giggle.

"Well, what is it? Whose past? What past?"

"Your past."

"Mine?"

"The German past," I say. "Your Nazi past. Germans coming to terms with the crimes they committed. During the Holocaust. Digesting it. Making amends."

Mick's looking at the train in front of us, nodding, like one of those dogs with a bobbing head that people put on the dashboards of their cars. "I see," he says, nodding, bobbing. "I see—interesting."

And then he's quiet.

Interesting? As if it were some sort of theory to accept or discard. Or— "Did you have another word for it?" I want to know. "For dealing with the past. And with anti-Semitism?"

He thinks about it. "No, not that I know of. No."

"So they don't . . . talk about it here?"

Mick runs his fingers through his hair. "The Nazis, they say, are in West Germany, but . . . that doesn't really make sense, does it?"

"No. Not really."

The train in front of us is about to leave, but neither of us gets up. We sit in silence while its doors shut, and it leaves the station, again revealing the Iron Curtain in all its monstrousness.

The three cardiologists (or are they?) from the Mitropa restaurant come dashing up the steps. They look pretty drunk. They watch the train leave, then turn around and stumble toward the train behind us.

"Boy, are they pissed!" Mick says.

Pissed. The woman in the camel's hair coat used a bunch of other words when she was talking about the men at the Intershop. *Trashed. Plastered. Tight.*

"You know how they say the Eskimos have a hundred words for snow?" I say.

"Uh-huh."

"And the Amazonians a hundred for the color green?"

"Yeah? I didn't know that."

"Well, the Germans have a hundred words for the word *drunk. Tight. Plastered. Trashed. Pissed.* We can go on and on."

"Well, that's better than English! You have only one word for everything. *Fuck*."

"Really? As far as I know it only means one thing."

Oops. There I go. Flirting again. Me and my potty mind.

"Listen to this," Mick begins. "The summer before last, I was at a Bruce Springsteen concert. In Weissensee. A little east of Prenzlauer Berg. Amazing! And afterward, thousands of us were roaming the streets, completely high on the Boss, and my friends and I passed some Americans, big black guys, soldiers."

Mick stands up, and he's suddenly this big black guy. He sways a little as if he were drunk. "They were completely fried—" He goes back to being Mick for a second. "Another one of your drunk words, huh? Anyway." He's the GI again now. "They were completely washed up and—" He giggles. "There was something wrong with their car. They couldn't get it started. A big Ford. And this guy was cursing all over the place. 'This fucking fuck won't fuck!' he yelled. 'Fuck it!' And this other guy tried to calm him down, and the big guy pushed him away and said, 'Fuck off.' And then the little guy said, 'Fuck you.' And the big guy said, 'Fuck yourself, you little fucker.' And I have to say, I learned a lot about the English language that night."

I'm laughing. Hysterically. That is so funny. I will have to tell Martha Rosen this one. She'll love it.

A train pulls up in front of us.

Mick sits back down, taken with his own performance.

I watch people coming up the steps and getting into the train behind us. In front of us, the train empties.

"When I was little," I say, "my mother used to walk me to school." I conjure up an image of Leonora. Tall, slender, so beautiful with her amazing silver hair. When the sun shone on it, it looked like diamonds had been sprinkled into her curls. Little sparkles of—

"You were saying?" says Mick, bringing me back to the here and now.

"We used to play a game, my mother and I. The adjective game. She taught languages. English. And German. And naturally she wanted me to have a good vocabulary. So if it was sunny out, she might say. 'Oh, what a beautiful day.' And then I'd substitute the adjective. 'Oh, what a pretty day,' I'd say. And then she'd say, 'Stunning,' and I'd say, 'Gorgeous.' She'd say, 'Fabulous,' and I'd say, 'Stupendous.' It went on and on. Sometimes we'd do it in English. And sometimes in German. English usually took longer because it has more words. More synonyms."

"Really?"

"Except for the adjective *drunk*, of course."

Mick is looking at me. It's very intense. For a moment I want to look away, but I hold his gaze. I wonder what he sees? Does he know I'm a wallflower, the girl no one asks to dance? Does he see the girl who lives in a crack? Too bad I wore this boyish flannel shirt today. I have more flattering clothes. Nothing like Carlotta's neon-pink tube dress, of course, but— Oh, he's smiling now, his head is tilted to the side, flirtatiously, and I see his slightly crooked teeth. I like them. And I smell his cedar scent again. And now—

"Your mother sounds nice," Mick says gently, almost carefully. I think he understands without asking that she's gone.

I nod. "She was." I gulp down some air. "She's dead. She passed away five years ago. It was cancer."

He thinks a moment before answering. I can tell he's trying

to find the right words. "It must have been tough for you," he says kindly. "Losing your mother at that age."

"It was."

He nods.

I stand up. "We better get that train," I say.

Ten

Berlin Alexanderplatz

The S-Bahn seats here aren't made of wooden slats—they're cushioned and upholstered in a gray-blue leatherette. Otherwise, both the East and the West S-Bahn look the same. And smell the same. I try to block out the disinfectant and concentrate on Mick's cedar scent. Occasionally I pick up a whiff of laundry detergent that continues to cling to the seams of my flannel shirt.

The train's crowded, but we find two seats beside each other, and before we know it, East Berlin is spooling by in shades of brown and beige and gray, building skeletons like ancient ruins, the river, bridges, and a cathedral loom ahead. The city looks majestic from up here. Crumbling, yes, but grand all the same.

"I can't believe I'm sitting with an American in the S-Bahn!" Mick blurts out. "I have a thousand questions."

I would like to view the scenery, but I can do that later, when I go back to West Berlin, by myself.

By myself. Funny—the thought makes me blue. Because of Mick? Yes, maybe. It was just two hours ago that I first saw him, yet the thought of having to say good-bye to him now saddens me.

"So you live in New York?" Mick says.

"In Manhattan. On Riverside Drive."

"Riv-er-side-drive. What river?"

"The Hudson," I say, though it seems odd to be talking about a river in New York when below us the River Spree is winding round a bend. "We can see across the Hudson to New Jersey."

Mick is listening with every cell of his body.

I try to envision it for the first time with his eyes: "From my window, you can see the factories that line the Jersey coast. Thick black smoke pours out of the chimneys. And there are high-rise apartment buildings near the waterfront. And behind it all, on a clear day, you can see the flat lay of the land for miles and miles. You would swear you can see all the way to Washington, to the White House, and beyond. Even Florida." I turn to Mick. "The view's spectacular. Especially when the sun sets."

"You're lucky," he says, reverently. "To live there."

Me? Lucky? I never thought of it like that. I always think of myself as being unlucky.

"New Jersey," he says, tasting it, feeling it, envisioning it. "Bruce Springsteen's from New Jersey. Amazing!"

I don't think it's that amazing, but who am I to judge?

"So you're in 'high school'?" Mick goes on. "That's what you call it, right?"

I nod.

"Do you walk to school?"

I have to laugh—he's so eager. "No. I usually take the subway. It's downtown. Near the World Trade Center."

"Have you ever been up there?"

"I have."

"And?" he wants to know.

"I suppose it's like being on top of your television tower," I say, gesturing out the window. "When you look down, the cars all look like tiny Legos."

The train pulls into Marx-Engels-Platz.

"We get off at the next stop," Mick says. "And then we switch to the subway." He's leaning forward, almost touching me.

"What kind of car do you have?"

"We don't have a car."

"Not even a Cadillac?"

I roll my eyes.

The two men sitting across from us are staring at us. One of them is reading a newspaper: *Berliner Zeitung*. It must be from the East as I'm not familiar with it. "CHANCELLOR KOHL'S BEATING AROUND THE BUSH" says a headline. The other man, dressed sensibly with one of those Russian-style fur hats with ear flaps, just looks at us, his face a blank.

"My father says it's too much trouble to have a car in the city," I say. "How do you know all about Cadillacs?"

Mick whispers. His breath is warm. And I close my eyes. I can feel his lips on my ear. "Because I watch West television."

"You were allowed to?" I whisper back.

"It was like West radio," he says. "It wasn't encouraged, but if you didn't talk about it, you were on the safe side. Everyone watched West TV."

"How do you know if no one talked about it?"

He thinks about this a moment. "We knew."

The two men are still staring at us. It's spooky. Three weeks ago we couldn't have talked about things like this in public. But nothing can happen now, can it? Even if they *were* policemen. Or the Stasi. It's over. And done with.

"It sounds like everyone was doing and thinking stuff they weren't supposed to be doing and thinking," I say. "It's sick."

If they ever make a movie about it, and they should, they could call it *The Virus from East Berlin*: *A very sick movie for very sick people. Featuring the smash hit: "Where Have All the Schizos Gone?"*

"Yeah," says Mick, "it *is* kind of sick."

"It's schizophrenic."

"Yeah."

"Well, don't worry about it," I say. "We have lots of therapists in the West."

Alexanderplatz, as seen from the elevated S-Bahn, is futuristic—a vast, gray, flat square, the television tower rising from its center like a rocket in a Cape Canaveral launchpad. It makes even *me* feel small.

"Stick with me," says Mick, taking my elbow and steering me past the throngs.

The platform is lined with people, and it's not even rush hour. I wouldn't go as far as to say Alexanderplatz is as busy as New York's Penn Station, but by Berlin standards it's teeming with life. I suppose if I were by myself, I'd pay attention to the signs directing me to the subway, but with Mick as my guide, I shift into cruise mode and let him do the piloting.

We walk down one flight of steps, wander through a huge drafty concourse, turn left, then right, go down more steps, trek through a tunnel, and come out into an underground area with mint-green tiled walls and a ceiling so low, if I weren't so self-conscious, I'd jump up and touch it with my fingertips.

"The subway," says Mick, a proud squire showing off the lovely gardens behind his country estate.

We pass a subterranean jewelry store and a souvenir shop with remarkably uncluttered windows, as if the proprietors were waiting for a shipment of wares that got lost at sea.

"I have to show you something," says Mick, his step quickening. I hurry to keep up as we weave through the crowd. I'm breathless, as if I were six years old and out jogging with my mother. Mick steers to the left, to a long wall where the souvenir shop ends.

"Come over here," he says, putting down the Legos. He walks right up to the wall, his chest, the palms of his hands, and his ear flush against it. "You, too."

I just look at him.

"Now!" he says with great urgency. "Hurry. Listen to this."

I feel silly, but I do it. I listen. And the wall actually seems to buzz.

"Do you hear the rumbling?" Mick asks.

I put my ear against the wall again. There's a lot of noise all around us, so I'm not so sure I *really* hear something behind the wall, but maybe Mick's ears are better than mine, the way my nose is better than his.

"The U8," Mick says, tapping the wall. "The BVG. The West subway."

"A train? Behind the wall?"

"Absolutely. The U8 passes through Alexanderplatz." He steps back and draws a line in the air straight through the hall. "Right here." Then he kicks the wall near the floor. "The steps to the platform are behind this." He points to a wall on the other side of the hall, opposite us. "And there too. They closed off the staircases."

I dip my hand into my pouch and pull out my BVG map. And there it is: Alexanderplatz, enclosed in a black rectangle, meaning it is unattainable with a West Berlin train. The U8, though, passes through it on its way north.

"It's a ghost station!" I say.

When I took the West subway with my ex-pal Carlotta and

her sister Marita to the Intershop at Friedrichstrasse, we had to ride through some ghost stations too, stops on the West subway that passed through East Berlin territory on the way north but were closed off from use because of the Berlin Wall. East Berliners couldn't get into those stations, and West Berliners couldn't get off the train. It was uncanny.

I remember an announcement came on over the platform loudspeaker at the station before East Berlin territory. "Kochstrasse. Last stop in West Berlin." It was like a threat: "Beware! If you dare to proceed, the Wicked Witch of the East may descend upon you." The doors closed, and the train, as I remember it, moved at a snail's pace. When we got into the first ghost station traveling north, Stadtmitte, we stood at the door, hoping to spot an East German border guard walking in and out of the shadows. Maybe we would even see a machine gun strapped across his shoulder. What we found was a gloomy, barely lit station with broken tiles, dirt and trash strewn about, everything marked by the heavy pall of dust and grime from twenty-eight years of neglect. And—yes!— over there, look, a guard with a—

"I was here last Sunday," Mick says. "Under here. In the West subway. It was eerie . . . So . . . unreal. My mother dropped me off at the subway. At Osloer Strasse. And I took it to Kreuzberg, to Kottbusser Tor. I rode right under here, under Alexanderplatz and through all those other ghost stations. Bernauer Strasse. Weinmeisterstrasse. I didn't even know they existed! Look, they're not on my map!" Mick takes his wallet out of the back pocket of his jeans and pulls out a folded transit map. It looks different than mine. "Do you see? Those stations aren't even on here," Mick says, unfolding it.

His map is confusing. The ghost stations and all the West

stations are missing. And all the East S-Bahn lines are in the same color green, and they don't have names like S3 or S1. And there are numbers along the lines that are puzzling.

"What are these numbers for?" I ask.

"That shows how long it takes to get somewhere. Here's Alexanderplatz," he says pointing to the station on his map. "And here's Schönhauser Allee. It takes eight minutes to get from here to there."

Only eight minutes? Does that mean that when Mick and I get on the subway, we'll be at Schönhauser Allee eight minutes later? And then we'll never see each other again?

Mick picks up his bag with the pirate Legos and points ahead. "That way."

We walk a few steps, and a breathtaking maze of staircases, escalators, banisters, and balustrades of wrought iron reveals itself. We turn right and start down an impossibly long flight of steps.

"Wait! This is wrong," says Mick. "This is to Hönow. Sorry."

I have no idea where we're going. I just follow Mick back up, turn right twice, go down a few more steps, and we're at the foot of a long walkway with shops right and left. We pass a stocking shop, a store with porcelain, and a large luggage and leather goods shop.

"Hey," says Mick, "my grandparents and I are thinking of getting my mother a suitcase set for Christmas. Do you mind if we go in for a second?"

I look at my watch. It's almost 1:30! I really have to get going. We keep on getting sidetracked. I wanted to be in Greifenhagener Strasse by now and—

"Stop looking at that watch!" Mick says.

"But—"

He puts his hand to my lips. "Shh," he says, and then takes hold of my elbow and steers me into the shop.

My lips tingle as if he had kissed me.

The shop is crowded, and the salespeople look busy. Mick puts the Legos down in a corner near a display with leatherette tote bags and appraises the suitcases while I look at the handbags. They're not very stylish. The leather is rough, and it smells sour, acidic, definitely not as aromatic as the leather I know. I pick up a brown leather purse, sniff it, and realize that Mick is staring at me. He comes over to me. "Don't let the saleslady see you do that," he says. "They don't like customers touching the goods."

"It smells funny," I say, putting the bag back in the display. "Did you see any suitcases?"

"Nah." Mick shakes his head, then points to the bag. "Leather always smells funny."

"No, not at all. Leather can also smell nice. It takes on odors easily. Your jacket, for instance."

"Yeah? What's it smell like?"

I know I'm getting red again. I feel the heat rush to my cheeks. It will burn off my eyelashes if I don't watch it. "It smells like cedar."

"You can smell that? It was in a cedar chest for fifty years! It was my great-grandfather's!"

Wow. I really *do* have a good nose. If I don't become a cook or a chemist like my father, maybe I should pursue a career in law enforcement and become a sniffer for the police department.

Mick models his jacket, turning right and left. "Notice the

fine workmanship on the buttonholes," he says, gesturing to them. "And the double-stitching on the collar."

This guy's hysterical!

"My great-grandfather died pretty young," Mick tells me. "Of pneumonia. When he was thirty-seven. My great-grandmother put all his stuff in a cedar chest. And when she died last year, my grandfather found the chest in her attic and gave me the jacket. It was actually a coat. But there were some holes in it. So we shortened it. And put in a new lining. Look!" He shows me the inside of the jacket where the lining has been stitched by hand. "I put in the lining."

"You?"

Mick nods.

"You *sewed* the lining? Yourself? By hand?" The stitches are perfect.

"Why not?"

"I just don't know any boys who sew. Definitely not like that."

He shrugs. "Everyone takes the subject needlework in school."

"Russian and needlework. What a combination."

"Survival of the fittest," says Mick dryly. "I knit too."

"I am impressed. Even I don't know how to knit."

"I can teach you," says Mick. "Then you can knit your father a scarf. I knit my mother one." He starts for the exit. "She was wearing it on Sunday when she dropped me off at the subway. That was some wild afternoon. She was going to visit an old school friend who lives in Wedding, near Osloer Strasse. So she gave me a lift into Berlin. We entered the city at the Bornholmer Strasse border control. She was bawling like a baby when the guards waved us through. It was the first time for her. The first time in twenty-eight years. She couldn't believe we had really crossed the border. I had to reach over and help her steer because she couldn't see where she was going."

Mick is laughing, remembering. "Her whole face was wet with tears. She was completely out of control. So we pulled over. We had to."

Mick and I are back in the subway walkway, standing in front of the luggage store. "My mother's really something!" he tells me. "You can't believe what she did. She opened up this box of test tubes she has in the car—the car's really for work and the test tubes are for, I don't know, bull semen. Or cow's blood. Milk samples. Whatever. So she took out a test tube, and she did the craziest thing. She let her tears drop into the tube, and then she put the stopper on it and wrote on the test tube, 'November 19, 1989, Berlin, Bornholmer Strasse.' And then she gave it to me and said, 'It's for your grandchildren.'"

"Wow. That's intense. That's like twenty-eight years of tears in a test tube."

"Nah. You'd be surprised. It wasn't that much. And it's all dried up now, anyhow. Evaporated."

He walks over to a stamping machine and validates two subway tickets. "My treat," he says, and winks at me. "Big spender. Twenty pfennigs." He watches the people rushing by a moment, then turns to me. "But I'm still going to save it. The test tube. And I'll give it to my grandchildren. I will."

When we get to the Alexanderplatz subway platform where the train to Pankow comes in, I'm still thinking about the test tube. And the tears. There was so much going on—right around the corner!—that I knew nothing about, never even thought about, never even *wanted* to think about. "Was last Sunday the first time you were in West Berlin?" I ask Mick.

"Are you joking? Of course not. I was there on November ninth when they opened up the border. At Sonnenallee."

"Sonnenallee?"

He looks at me as if I were an alien. And maybe I am.

"In Neukölln," Mick says.

Oh. Neukölln. I was there once. A few months ago. On a warm September afternoon. With Bo Brody and Edda. Bo was dying to show me where they used to live, right at the Wall, with a view of the East. In front of their old house, we climbed up one of those wooden observation towers that dot the border on the West side. We could see over the wall where there was a wide strip of no-man's-land, then a paved road, then a high fence with barbed wire behind it, and behind that an apartment house. There were people at a window looking at us. Edda waved. Which was a little silly, I thought.

The people at the window probably thought so too. But then a Jeep with East German border guards rode by, and the people at the window disappeared into the shadows of their apartment.

After that we walked along the Wall, looked at the graffiti, and watched this girl punk spray flowers in green and purple on the Wall. Two kids were playing squash, and they lost their ball when it flew over the Wall. No way were they going to go after it. At a corner pub, there was a group of people celebrating a wedding. Dancing at the Wall. Business as usual.

We're standing near a newspaper stand. I see our reflection in the kiosk's glass. Two giants among midgets: one an East Berliner, the other an alien.

A train on the other track rumbles into the station.

"You want to buy one?" Mick asks, pointing to the newspaper stand. "As a souvenir?"

They have newspapers and magazines I've never seen before. A weekly called *Wochenpost*, *Sibylle*, which is a women's magazine, and *Bummi*, a magazine for kids. I can buy Gwen the *Sibylle*.

"Good idea," I say, walking up to the counter. But a woman behind the glass window, counting money, shoos us away with an irritable "Are you blind?" She points to a sign in the window: *"Bitte nicht stören—Schichtübergabe."* Don't disturb—shift rotation.

Mick and I simultaneously look heavenward, then lean back against a wall and wait for our train. That woman, like the waiter in the Mitropa, is definitely not on our team!

"Tell me more about November ninth," I say.

"What do you want to know?"

I want to know everything, but there's no time for that, is there? "Why Sonnenallee?" I ask. "Why not Brandenburger Tor or Checkpoint Charlie or—"

"Because I was in Schöneweide," says Mick. "At my uncle's. All the way in the south. I stay down there during the week because it's near my school. It's too far to go home to Birkenwerder every night." He looks at me, trying to figure out if I remember where Birkenwerder is. He decides I don't, which is correct. "Birkenwerder's all the way up north. It's not even Berlin. So on the ninth we were doing some extra scene work after class. I'm working on Konstantin from Chekhov's *The Seagull*—do you know it?"

Uh-oh. A gap in my education. "Not yet," I say wisely. "I promise to read it as soon as I get home this evening."

"Good."

Does he actually *believe* me?

"After rehearsal we hung around a little," he goes on, "had a beer or two, and then I went to my aunt and uncle's house. They were out, but my cousin was there, André. He's in the eighth grade. He'd just finished his homework, and we turned on the TV. And we couldn't believe our eyes. It was everywhere. All over television. Every station. The Wall was open! No one expected it. We grabbed our bikes and went to the border at Sonnenallee to see if it was really open. And it was! The barriers were up. The gates open. The border guards were just standing around looking like they had no idea what was happening. They just let us ride right past them. And one second later, we were in West Berlin. It was incredible. Like in the TV series *Star Trek*. Beam me up, Scotty. And there we were."

Mick breathes in deeply.

"And?" I say. "More. More. Tell me more."

"Okay. There were people on the West side. Neuköllner. They had champagne. And they cheered us when we came through. This old man came over to me and hugged me. 'I can't believe it,' he said. He repeated it over and over again. 'I can't believe it. I can't believe it.' He was hugging me so tight, I couldn't breathe. And then finally he let me go. And there were tears in his eyes. And that's when I knew that we were making history. No. No, it was more than just making history. We *were* history. All of us. Together. We were the history. We are the history."

Mick leans back against the Wall and smiles. "We hung out awhile," he says, "and then we biked up the Sonnenallee. It's a long street. It goes all the way up to Kreuzberg. And there it was, like a dark, long, gloomy tunnel. It's not exactly how you picture the West. We didn't see any advertisements. Or movie theaters. Or pubs. There was no one out on the street! It was just those housing projects that we can see from the East, anyway, from the S-Bahn. We went down some side streets where there were little houses with little gardens, and it looked just like Birkenwerder. Like anywhere in the East. At least in the dark. After a while we just turned around and went home. I have to admit it was a little disappointing. But the next day, we all went to Brandenburg Gate, stood on top of the Wall, and got really sloshed—" He socks me in my arm with a laugh. "There's another one of your drunk words. *Sloshed.*"

I give him a half smile.

"But as long as I live, when people ask me, 'Where were you on November ninth?' I'll say, 'I took the bike into Neukölln. And it was beautiful.' And it was. Kind of." He exhales, long and deep. "And you?" he asks. "What'd you do?"

"I slept through it. More or less."

"You're joking."

I shrug. "I'm a sound sleeper," I say. And for the first time in my life, I really, really wish I weren't.

Eleven

The Secret Life of Molecules

Red lights blink on and off, a shrill bell rings, the doors shut tight, the train jerks forward, and we have eight minutes until Schönhauser Allee. I watch the news kiosk fly by. Mick is sitting to my right. When I look down, our feet, in the black lace-up paratrooper boots, look like they belong to the same four-legged creature. The red sauce from the *Ketwurst* has dried on the toe of my right shoe. The left heel of Mick's boot is chipped. I wonder if it's a size twelve too.

Mick changes his position, and I hear the black leather of his jacket squeak and crunch. Our shoulders, arms, hips, and thighs are touching now. That's how close we're sitting. When I close my eyes and block everything else out, I feel the heat of his body next to mine. My coat is open, and my neck feels so naked, so vulnerable. I wonder what it would feel like if Mick kissed it. Right under my ear . . . I hardly ever wondered about things like that when I was with Oliver.

The train propels us forward toward Prenzlauer Berg. This is the last leg of our journey. Am I blue? Possibly. Possibly a lot. But I'm also relieved that this little interlude is over. Knowing that when we say good-bye it will be for the last time is zapping my energy. It's—

"I have three more questions," Mick says.

Better questions than good-byes. "Okay."

"Why, actually, are you going to Prenzlauer Berg?"

"And the second question?"

"What exactly does your father do? What's a theoretical chemist?"

I roll my eyes.

"Come on! I like complicated things," he says.

"And the third?" I ask.

"First answer one and two."

"Okay," I say, "number two first. It's less complicated than the first question and, contrary to you, I don't like complicated things." I turn to Mick, and our knees are touching now too. How do I explain this so he understands? "My father's not the kind of chemist who wears a white lab coat or carries out dangerous experiments that could blow up the block. He just . . . thinks."

"About?"

"Molecules. He uses physics, math, computers, whatever, to help us understand how molecules, how two or more atoms, bond chemically. He simulates molecular phenomena and predicts the properties of new molecules and—" I look at Mick. "Are you still with me?"

He nods.

"His head is full of numbers, formulas, equations, ideas. Sometimes in the middle of breakfast, he'll just get up and write something down. He's always sorting out his thoughts. He walks around with six different colored pencils in his breast pocket to keep it all organized. In his bathrobe too. They're all lined up. You should see his notebooks. Actually, they're wild, very colorful."

The train rolls into Rosa-Luxemburg-Platz. A blond couple, holding hands, climbs in and sits opposite us. They're beautiful. Pale. Fragile. I think they're in love. In any case, it's how I imagine love should look. I have a hard time taking my eyes away from them.

"It's like my father wants to be the first boy on the block to discover something new," I say. "A new theory, a new equation, a new concept."

Mick, I see, is taking peeks at the blond couple too.

"Afterward," I say, "other people can figure out what to do with his discoveries, but first it's my father's job to prove that his theory works. And he won't stop until he does." Mick nods to let me know he's still with me. "It can drive you crazy. He's very intense. And not always very communicative. At least once a week my mother wanted to throw him out of the house."

"Is he like the Einstein of chemistry?"

"No. At least I don't think so. He kind of slowed down a little after my mother died. But he's trying to catch up. He's working on—"

A sudden movement catches our attention. The blond couple opposite us, we now see, are deaf. Or at least one of them is. They're using sign language.

"He's working on something that deals with the laser control of . . . chemical reactions," I go on. "It's a . . . fairly . . . new field . . ."

I'm mesmerized by the couple. Their sign language is so extreme. Their eyes are eating each other up. Their smiles seem to leap off their lips and kiss each other. Their hands shift furiously in an amazing dance. I am staring. I know. And Mick is too. In fact, most everyone in the train is watching them now, pretending not to, fascinated by the loud silence of their dialogue, their hands whipping through the air, whooshing, fluttering, fists tapping their chests, knuckles knocking their heads. Their gestures are a whirlwind, their laughter a volcano. Their love is so huge, it fills up the whole train. Yes, I think, that is how I want to love too. Yes!

I look at Mick. And he looks at me.

"I'd like to meet your father," he says.

And it breaks my heart. Because he will never meet Fritz. How? I'm standing with one foot out the door.

"Tell me about Thanksgiving dinner," he says, leaning back.

"Is that the third question?"

He just smiles.

Tell me about Thanksgiving dinner. Is it possible that what he's really asking is, *Will you invite me to your party tonight?* Maybe he's waiting for me to say, *Why don't you come home with me, and then you'll see what Thanksgiving is all about . . .* I could invite him . . . but . . . no! The Blond Nightmare in Neon Pink will be there. Carlotta Schmidt. She'd steal him away before we even got to the stuffing. And then I'd leave Berlin even more unhappy than I already am. No. It's better we say good-bye now. At Schönhauser Allee. Short, painless, final.

The train enters the station Senefelderplatz. Four minutes to go.

I feel Mick's eyes on me. He wants an answer. He wants to know about Thanksgiving. I look at the deaf couple to buy a few seconds' time. But they've stopped signing. I feel like they're waiting for my answer too. They're sitting, very still, hands clasped, happily watching us. Watching me and Mick. What do they see? A giant and a giantess? The pirate and his lady? A wildflower and his wallflower? It's hard to know. But they're smiling. At us. As if they knew us. As if we were all on the same team. Is it possible that they think Mick and I are in love too?

"Let's get off," I say, getting up. "I need to tell you something."

Twelve

Confessions of an East German

"**They were something else,** weren't they?" Mick says of the deaf couple. He knows something's cooking. He's stalling for time. He throws me a jaunty smile. "I could have watched them for hours. What's up?" He plops down on a bench, long legs and long arms jutting out in all directions.

Not far from us, a subway attendant shouts, "Zurückbleiben" into a microphone. I wince when I hear it. They say it in the West too, just before the doors close—"Stay back!" I suppose it's for our own good, but it always sounds so bossy. Isn't there a nicer way to say, "Mind the closing doors?"

I watch the subway attendant put the microphone back into a column-like contraption that's almost as high as he is and then disappear into a little house in the middle of the platform.

Mick's looking at me. Waiting. He suddenly seems less self-confident than earlier.

"I'm leaving Berlin," I say. "On Saturday."

"Yeah? Where to?"

"New York."

His smile disappears as if I had turned it off with the flick of a switch. I stare at the tiled walls, at the sign SENEFELDER-PLATZ, waiting. Waiting for what?

Finally, he breaks the stillness. "I thought you said you were staying a year." His voice has an irritated edge to it.

"I said my *father* was staying a year."

Mick makes a face, a let's-not-quibble-over-words face. "I'm sorry," I say. "I didn't deliberately lead you on. I . . . I . . ." I *what?* I don't know. My life is full of ellipses. "I'm sorry," I say again.

The words float around in the chilly air a moment or two before settling on Mick's shoulders. He shrugs them off. "You don't owe me an apology. We just met."

The problem is I feel that I *do* owe him an apology. Somewhere back there we promised each other something. We promised each other the possibility that we might be friends. Maybe even more than friends. We never said it, but it was a promise all the same.

On the other track, the train to Otto-Grotewohl-Strasse via Alexanderplatz charges in. I have a sudden vision that Mick will shoot up and vanish into the train, that I'll never see him again. The thought is so distressful, that I reach out and take his hand—just in case. Mick turns to me, surprised.

Behind us the train leaves the station, and the subway attendant, at his microphone, whisks off. He's wearing a bunch of keys on his belt. They jingle. I feel Mick's eyes on me.

"You're my second rejection in less than twenty-four hours," he says.

His hand is very warm in my hand. I turn to him. "I'm not rejecting you."

"That's what it feels like."

Rejection. The story of *my* life.

"Who else . . . rejected you?" I ask.

"Elfi," he says, his eyes on the wall in front of him. "My ex. It was already over. But . . ."

He doesn't finish his sentence. It's good to know that he speaks in ellipses sometimes too.

"Is she the reason why you missed school today?" I ask.

Mick doesn't answer immediately. And it's ridiculous, I know, but I feel this awful thing, sharp, like little jagged teeth, pricking inside me. What is it? It could be that I'm just hungry. But, no, I'm not really hungry. It's something else. It's . . . jealousy, I think. I have no right, but, yes, I think I'm jealous. Of this Elfi. She sounds pretty. Petite. Coquettish. Everything I'm not.

"It was already over," mumbles Mick. He releases my hand and runs his fingers through his hair impatiently. "Months ago. We split in August. But yesterday it was . . . finalized. It was pretty emotional. And then I got smashed—" He breaks off his sentence and gives me a sidelong look. "Put that one on your list, Miss Lenzfeld. *Smashed.*"

I give him a half smile.

"We were supposed to go camping together," says Mick. "In August. With two other friends. To Hungary." He looks at me. "Hungary?"

Is that an insult or is that an insult? "I may be an uneducated American," I say, "but I *do* happen to know that there's a country called Hungary!"

"I didn't mean it like that!" Mick protests. "I just didn't know if you knew what was happening there in the summer."

"Oh. Okay, tell me what was happening."

"Hungary is one of the countries GDR citizens were allowed to travel to without a visa. And last spring the Hungarians opened up their border to Austria. By the time summer rolled around, thousands of East German citizens were using the open border to emigrate illegally to the West." He looks to see if I'm following him. I am. "And that's what Elfi wanted to do. With me. And with Bambi and Till, two buddies from Oranienburg."

Of course! Fritz and I saw it on the news the first week we got to Berlin. And we talked about it in school last week in social studies, when we made a list of the events leading up to the fall of the Wall. But East Germany had seemed so far away, as if it were in another solar system, not just around the corner. And here I am now, sitting on a bench in an East Berlin subway station with someone who was actually thinking of emigrating. It's so full of drama, so adult-like, so not the life of the teenagers I know—not that I know all that many very well, anyway.

"But I decided against it," says Mick. "And she went. Bambi and Till too."

"Jeez," I say. "That must have been such a hard decision for you."

He's nodding again like one of those dashboard dogs with the bobbing heads.

Behind me I hear the *clickety-click* of a woman on high heels coming toward us. I look up and—oh!—I think it's a *he*, a transvestite. At least that's what he looks like. He's all dolled up, as if he were off to a rehearsal for the *Rocky Horror Picture Show*. Out of habit, I take a look at his shoes. Size twelve, I believe. But they're lovely—dark red patent leather heels with straps that crisscross in front and clasp on the side. Amidst all the gray of the East, the color dazzles like sunlight.

The transvestite sashays past us, smiling. He looks vaguely familiar, but the moment is fleeting. *Clickety-click* go his heels, and he's gone. Mick waits for him to get out of earshot before he begins again. "Elfi had to leave most of her stuff at home. She only took a backpack. But she didn't get along with her stepmother and was afraid some stuff might get lost. So before she left, she gave me some keepsakes, in case we were ever to meet again."

I feel cool air on my right cheek. A train is coming in from Alexanderplatz. I hear its rumbling. And then it's upon us. Passengers exit. Passengers, like the transvestite, climb in. Red lights flash. A bell rings. The doors close. The train departs.

The station is quiet again.

"So that's what I did yesterday," Mick goes on. "I brought her the stuff back. Some teacups that belonged to her mother, a couple of books and cassettes, posters. A Dead Kennedys album. Her teddy bear." He laughs. "Her new boyfriend was there. Volker. Her *new* teddy bear. A taxi driver. From Schöneberg. Things got a little out of hand. I had too much to drink. And I conked out on the living room sofa. In her aunt's apartment. She's staying with her. In Charlottenburg."

"Did you expect her to . . . take you back?"

"Nah. It was over."

A wave of . . . relief—yes, relief—swells up in me. I have no right to be jealous. Or relieved. But I am.

"It was over even before August," says Mick. "But it was emotional, anyway. And she's still a little bitter."

"Because you wouldn't go with her?"

"That, plus she got a bad deal. One of the reasons why she left in the first place was because she couldn't study what she wanted to. She wanted to major in German, maybe work in publishing, but she was rejected. Instead, they offered her a place in education to become a Russian and German teacher. Russian! 'Honorable comrade, best wishes on the occasion of International Woman's Day.' If there was one thing Elfi didn't want to do, it was teach Russian."

"You can't decide for yourself what you want to study?"

"Sure you can. But who says you're going to get it? There's only a certain amount of spots, and if they're taken, they're taken." Mick turns to me. "When you think about it, it makes some sense. Why study medicine if there are already enough doctors? It's a waste of a good education. Better to be a nurse and have work. Look at Volker. He studied sociology. And? He's driving a cab."

"But if you don't want to be a nurse?"

He shrugs. "Then you've got a problem."

"Clearly a lot of East Germans had a problem. Still have one. Or . . . ?"

Mick runs his hand through his hair. I think he does this when he's uneasy. "I know. And if the Wall were still up, I probably would too. If not today, then tomorrow. But in August I didn't. Sure—I knew a lot wasn't working the way it should. But some stuff was okay. I had a happy childhood. Friends. A warm bed. I had enough—"

"Mick, you don't have—"

"I had enough to eat! I definitely had as much cabbage as I wanted."

Is he being funny?

"And apples! I had apples coming out of my ears. And eggs! Dripping out of my nose. And of course as much milk as I wanted!"

"You don't have to defend yourself!"

"Yes, I do!"

Ouch! He sounds upset now.

"I *do* have to defend myself. You want to know why I stayed. Elfi wants to know why I stayed. *I* want to know why I stayed. My grandchildren will want to know why I stayed when I give them that test tube from my mother. So I've been thinking about it. Okay? Since August. Maybe—"

A woman, walking by with two children, gives us a wide

berth. Mick notices. Embarrassed, he stops talking mid-sentence and lowers his voice. "Maybe I stayed because I'm not a hero," he says. "Or maybe because I'm easy to satisfy. Or maybe because I'm too young and don't know better. For all I know, maybe I stayed because I *am* a hero. I don't know. All I know is that I have what I want. I love the theater. I wanted to study acting. I can't think of anything else I'd like to do more. And I got the chance to do it. You don't just throw something like that away." He crosses his arms around his chest, and his jacket squeaks. And then crunches. "And my family was here," he says. "And the world was starting to come to us. Bruce Springsteen was here. Bob Dylan. We were starting to demonstrate. I was in Leipzig for the Monday demonstrations. We thought maybe we could change things." His fingers are running wildly through his hair. "I don't know. What would you have done, Molly?"

Mick's looking at me, but I think his question is rhetorical. I don't think he really wants an answer. I shrug, anyway, because now that I think about it, I actually *don't* know what I would have done.

"There are a lot of reasons why I stayed," he sums up. "Plus, I didn't have to go to the army, so—"

"Why not actually?"

Mick's fingers are running furiously through his hair.

Another train is about to come in on the Otto-Grotewohl side of the platform. We hear the distant drum roll. The attendant, on his way to the head of the platform, clears his throat as he passes our bench. "Everything in order?" he asks, curious, authoritarian, stern, arrogant—all of it, all at once.

"Perfect!" says Mick, cheerfully. He really is a good actor.

The man, though, doesn't seem thoroughly convinced. *Are*

they trouble or not? he's thinking. He tries not to look at our paratrooper boots. And I try not to look at his footwear but do. He has tiny feet and is wearing those soft shoes that old people run around in, beige, with little ventilation holes so your feet can breathe. He's not old, though. He can't be more than forty. "Can I help you?" he says, but the way he says it, it sounds like *What the hell are you two doing here?* "Loitering is not permitted—"

"We're fine! Thanks!" says Mick with a smile that stretches all the way from Senefelderplatz to Savignyplatz.

The man, taken aback by Mick's cheerfulness, nods, then scampers away, his keys jingling.

Mick picks up the thread of our conversation. "The People's Army rejected me," he says. "That's why I didn't go." He gives me a smile. "It's more complicated than theoretical chemistry."

"Shoot."

"My eyes were almost reason enough to get me out of it," he says. "But not quite. When I was a kid, my left eye was much weaker than the right one, so I had to wear a patch over the right one, so the left one would get stronger. Now both are weak—equally. Strictly speaking, though, I shouldn't have been rejected because of it. But I was." He jumps up. "Look at me! Do you understand it? I don't. I'm just lucky! It's a mystery!"

Actually, I *can* understand it. There's something so exuberant about Mick. You can't not like him. I bet all the girls are crazy about him. Not just Elfi.

"My stroke of luck was that the doctor who did the physical happened to know my grandfather. Plus, he was in the mood to do a good deed that day. The good deed was saving three years of my life."

108

"Wow."

"Things were already getting fuzzy. Falling apart. People were taking risks. So he took one too. I owe him a lot—three years of my life. I'm giving him a front-row seat when I get my first role." He sits down again. "So that's it. The story of my life. The confessions of an East German."

"It sounds like the title for a movie." I put on one of those off-camera voices you hear on movie trailers: "Confessions of an East German: A docudrama about life, love, and strife behind the Wall."

"Nah. I'm not so sure I want to be in that movie." Mick jumps up again, holds out his hand, and pulls me up. "Come on. We have to get you to Prenzlauer Berg. It's almost two."

As I have already mentioned, Mick has a strong grip.

I hold on tight.

Thirteen

From Berlin with Love

The train is surprisingly empty. The shoppers are out shopping, and the rush hour has yet to come. Some people are sitting at the other end of the car, but otherwise we're alone.

The bell rings. The red lights flash. We're off.

Mick and I are leaning against the door, still holding on to each other, hands clasped. Like lovers. Like the deaf couple. If we don't watch out, we'll be talking sign language with each other too, smiles bouncing off our faces and landing in the other's lap or something.

My fingertips tingle now in Mick's hand. Maybe because we know that in four minutes we'll arrive at Schönhauser Allee and say good-bye; maybe that has given us the license to act like we're on a date. Maybe Mick will put his hand under my hood again and pull me toward him. Maybe we'll kiss. Maybe he'll come visit me in New York. Maybe—

"You never answered my first question," says Mick.

"And you never asked the third."

"First the first."

"Which was?"

"Why are you going to Prenzlauer Berg?"

Our lips are so close, we could kiss. I see a distorted reflection of my face in the thin sliver of his silver loop earring. I breathe in his cedar scent. My eyes scan the dark shadows on his cheek, tiny little hairs breaking through the surface of his skin. What would he do if I reached out and grazed his cheek with my fingertips? Or brushed my lips against his ear? Or took off his glasses and kissed one weak eye and the other weak eye? Or—

"Molly?"

Mick is grinning. I hope he doesn't have to straighten his teeth for his career. A crooked tooth here and there gives a good actor personality.

"Yes?" I say.

"Why Prenzlauer Berg?"

I rarely talk about Leonora. But his question sounds so insistent. Not in a bad way. But as if he really cares and won't stop asking until I satisfy him with an answer.

Our eyes meet. Yes, he's determined to hear an explanation. I brace myself for an emotional roller-coaster ride.

"My mother lived there," I say. "Until she was almost seven. On Greifenhagener Strasse. I wanted to see her birth house before I left Berlin."

"Your mother? Really? Wow."

He seems so relieved. What on earth did he think? That I was visiting a boyfriend?

"When did she move away?" Mick wants to know. "Before they put up the Wall?"

I almost laugh. "Nineteen thirty-eight."

Mick is genuinely surprised. "That's even before the war! Were your grandparents anti-fascists? Is that why they left?"

Again I have to curb an impulse to laugh—but I suppose his reaction is typical for someone who grew up in East Germany. "My grandparents were Jewish, Mick. That's why they left."

"Oh. Right."

Ouch! We're suddenly blitzed by glaring light. The train

has emerged from underground and is starting up an incline. I didn't realize that the subway is elevated here. I squint at the colorless city below us, at tones of brown, beige, and gray dappled in sunlight. Prenzlauer Berg.

"I never met anyone who was Jewish," says Mick, running his fingers through his hair again.

"Maybe they were and you just didn't know?"

"Maybe." He thinks about it a moment. "They didn't advertise it. That's for sure."

"We talked about it every day. Well—every other. My mother was pretty ambivalent. Toward Germany. To both Germanys, I guess. But my father's not Jewish."

"But German??"

I nod. "His father died in the war. Let's say he didn't mind my mother's ambivalence. But I think he missed Germany. *West* Germany. He seems perfectly happy in Berlin now."

"You never visited Germany? Don't you have family here?"

"Most of my mother's relatives emigrated. A few didn't and were . . . murdered. My father's mother, my grandmother, died before I was born. My father has a couple of cousins. But they visit *us*. New York is slightly more interesting than Hünfeld."

Mick grins. "I wouldn't know."

"What? You haven't been to Hünfeld yet?"

"It's at the top of my list of things to do," Mick says dryly. "Right after New York."

I wonder what it would be like to stroll down Fifth Avenue with Mick on a beautiful spring day. Or ride the New York subway with him. I'm sure he'd get a kick out of how it screeches. Maybe we could walk across the Brooklyn Bridge together and then—

112

The train stops. Dimitroffstrasse. Just two minutes to Schönhauser Allee.

"I think my mother would have come to Germany, if she had lived," I say. "Especially now. With the Wall."

"So you came for her," he says kindly.

"Maybe." I shrug. "But I don't think of it that way."

I'm surprised at how easy it is for me to talk about Leonora. I start breathing again.

"Today, though, is for her," I say. "I'm on a mission."

There it is. I've said it. *I'm on a mission.*

"A mission? Like James Bond?" he says.

How does he know about James Bond? From West television? "Yeah," I say. "Like a regular agent 007. *From Berlin with Love.*"

"Brief me," he quips.

Where to begin? I take in a deep breath.

"My mother liked to talk about her house on Greifenhagener Strasse," I say. "Even in the end, when she was sick, when she was dying, she talked about it." My voice is beginning to quiver. Maybe this isn't as easy as I thought. "And she used to talk about a garden plot that was in the courtyard. How everyone helped plant it. And how they built a stone wall to keep the neighbors' chickens out because the chickens were pecking away at the flowers. She loved to describe how everyone helped build the wall. Stone by stone. The kids too. And how they all played out there in the summer. Children came from all over the neighborhood to duck under the sprinkler." I look at Mick. "I think that's what she missed most when she left Germany. That camaraderie. That feeling of belonging. And she felt . . . betrayed somehow. All these people who were a part of who she was . . . betrayed her."

Mick grasps my hand tighter, and my throat feels as if a lump of charcoal just got stuck in it. I turn to the window, watch the gray tones of Prenzlauer Berg reel by. I inhale. Exhale. "Anyway," I go on, "my sister Gwen asked me if I would bring her back a piece of the Berlin Wall. And our neighbor, Bo, he went to Checkpoint Charlie and chiseled some away for her. And then I thought I should bring my mother back something too . . ." It's getting harder to talk now. I squeeze my eyes shut in the vain attempt to hold back the tears. "I wanted to bring her something. From Berlin. From her homeland. But the Berlin Wall didn't seem appropriate—that's all a part of what betrayed her, right?"

Mick nods, intent on listening.

"And then I had this idea," I say, "that I would go to her birth house and bring her back a piece of the garden wall that she had helped build as a little girl." I look up at Mick. "There's a Jewish tradition that after you visit a grave you put a stone or a pebble on the grave site before you leave. It's symbolic for saying that we're never finished building a monument to the deceased, never finished honoring the memory of this person who once lived."

"I never knew that," says Mick, gently.

"And it's also a way of marking the grave," I say, my voice struggling now, "so other people who come by see that here lie the remains of someone who was loved and who is worthy of remembrance. And if anyone was loved and worthy of remembrance, it was my mother." The tears are streaming down now. "So that's what I'm going to do. I hope the wall is still standing, and then I'm going to chisel off a piece of it and bring it home and put it on my mother's grave."

Mick releases my hand. He's searching his pockets for a

tissue. I fumble around in my pouch looking for one too. My fingers brush against something hard. And metallic. "Look!" I say, and pull out a hammer. And then a chisel. "You see?"

I don't know if I'm laughing or if I'm crying now. I think both. And it feels . . . I'm not sure. It feels . . . okay. No. It feels better than okay. It feels good. It does. It feels good to cry like this. And to laugh. And to—

The train stops, and I realize we're no longer outside but underground again.

Mick looks up. "Shit! Pankow! The last stop! We went one station too far!" He's pointing to the other side of the platform where a train is already waiting for its return trip. We dash across the platform, practically banging into a man with a saxophone case strapped across his shoulder. His hat falls off. "Where's the fire?" he calls out. But he's not angry, just startled.

"Sorry!" we shout back, and leap into the train just before the doors close.

There are just a couple of people in this car too. We lean against the door. Mick hands me a tissue. My eyes are still wet, I guess. I dab them dry. "Thanks, Mick."

Mick takes my hands in his. "I know it sounds strange, but . . . thanks too."

It doesn't sound strange. I think I know what he's saying. I think he wants me to know that it makes him feel good that I trusted him with my mother's story.

We're outside again. It's not sunny out, but I feel lighter.

We stare at each other a couple of seconds, then Mick breaks the silence. "I need to tell you something too."

Uh-oh. This doesn't sound good. It sounds like he has a girlfriend. Post-Elfi. My levity disappears.

"You know how you said before that I smelled like cedar?" he says.

I'm confused. What does a new girlfriend have to do with cedar? "What about it?" I ask.

"You smell good too."

What on earth is he talking about?

"Now, don't laugh, okay?" he says.

It's really hard not to laugh when you're talking about how people *smell*. "I'll try not to," I say. "But—"

"I noticed you right off, on the S-Bahn, at Savignyplatz. But you looked away."

I shrug, remembering that his eyes were so penetrating, so intense.

"I thought you looked interesting," he says. "You know, the usual—pretty, nice haircut, cool boots."

"Ha-ha."

"Quiet in the peanut gallery. But it was something else that made me wait outside the checkpoint for you."

This is beginning to sound interesting. My heart thinks so too. It's racing away. In fact, it's moving so fast, it'll get to Schönhauser Allee before our train does.

"You smell like the West," he says.

"I smell like the West?"

"Like an Intershop."

"Like an Intershop?"

This has got to be the most *un*romantic thing I have ever heard in my entire life. I smell like an Intershop? All I can think of are those drunks at the Intershop and their sour smell.

Mick is laughing. "Yes! It's a compliment, Molly! Believe me! Intershops are the epitome of . . . of . . . longing. Desire. Hope. The Golden West. We craved the smell of the Intershop."

116

I'm sorry. But if this is a confession of love, it doesn't really work. But I will give Mick the benefit of the doubt.

"What does an Intershop smell like?" I want to know.

"Like . . . tobacco. And . . . gum. Spearmint gum. Coffee. Maybe chocolate. And . . ." Mick inhales, leans toward me, and breathes in the scent of my hair, my coat, my neck. *This*, I have to say, is romantic. More than romantic. It's *sexy*.

"Here," he says, sniffing my shirt collar. "Right here! You smell like . . . laundry detergent. *West* laundry detergent."

West laundry detergent?! This is even more unromantic than smelling like an Intershop!

Two boys with backpacks are staring at us. They turn to each other and start sniffing their clothes, giggling, imitating us.

The train stops. Schönhauser Allee.

"Yeah," says Mick, pulling open the door and guiding me out to the platform. "West laundry detergent. I smelled it in the S-Bahn. When we were both crawling on the floor picking up the Legos and—"

"Oohh!" we gasp.

"The Legos!" Mick cries out. "Shit!"

The bag with the Legos is gone!

Fourteen

Pretty in Pink

We jump back into the train, but the Legos aren't there. The doors close.

"Did we leave them in Pankow?" Mick asks, flustered. "On the platform?"

I try to remember. "I don't think so."

"David and Viktor are going to kill me! *I'm* going to kill me!" says Mick. His fingers are running uneasily through his hair. "Shit!"

"Maybe we left it on the *train* to Pankow," I say. "Is there a lost-and-found somewhere?"

"Or at the Senefelderplatz station?" says Mick. "At the bench?"

When I envision us sitting on the bench at Senefelderplatz, I don't see the bag.

"Maybe on the train from Alexanderplatz *to* Senefelder-platz," I say, but then I remember looking down and seeing only our boots. There was no bag either. "Before that. We lost it before that."

"The Mitropa in Friedrichstrasse?"

I shake my head. "No you had it when you brought me the *Ketwurst* after we were in the Mitropa. And I remember it on the S-Bahn to Alexanderplatz. And it was next to us when we listened to the U8 in the subway. And—"

"The leather shop!" we say practically in unison.

Yes! Mick put the bag down next to the totes in the leather shop! Exactly!

We lean back against the door, relieved. The Legos are most likely safe in the store.

"You don't have to go all the way back with me," Mick says. "Get off the next stop and take the next train back to Schönhauser Allee. I can meet you at the house. On Greifenhagener Strasse."

"You want to come with me?"

I feel light. Buoyant. If I could get rid of a couple of pounds—maybe take off my boots and my coat—and magically change the laws of gravity, I bet I would float away on this cloud of . . . of what? Happiness? Joy? Euphoria?

"Of course I want to come!" Mick says. "I wouldn't miss you hammering and chiseling down a wall for anything."

"*Attack of the Fifty-Foot Woman.*"

"Huh?"

"Forget it. American culture. It's even more complicated than theoretical chemistry."

Our smiles are leaping off our faces like they did with the deaf couple. If those two schoolboys weren't sitting there, staring at us, I might kiss Mick. "But don't you have to go to Birkenwerder?" I say. Okay—it's a rotten alternative to a kiss, but I'm not the most versed in situations such as this.

Mick swats the question away. "Unimportant."

Unimportant. He wants to spend time with me. And I want to spend the last minutes with him too.

The train is crawling into the earth now. In a moment we'll be back underground and about to pull into Senefelderplatz.

"I'm going back with you to Alexanderplatz," I say. "It's just a couple of minutes more."

"Are you sure?" he says.

The train stops at Senefelderplatz. I stay put. "Yes, I'm sure," I say. Maybe I should even invite him to Thanksgiving dinner. The way I feel now, I think I can weather a hurricane called Carlotta.

"Look!" Mick grabs my hand and pulls me over to the door across from us. The subway attendant with the ventilation shoes is there, holding his microphone. Mick knocks on the window to get his attention. The man frowns at us and scurries back to his burrow. He's not on our team either.

Mick and I lean back against the door, laughing. When was the last time I laughed like this? It feels great—like sneezing six times in a row.

We don't stop laughing until we get to Rosa-Luxemburg-Platz. By then I'm almost ready to invite Mick to Thanksgiving dinner. I really like him. And he makes me like *me*. He makes me like who I am when I'm with him. He makes me think that—

Oh. Mick takes my hand . . . raises it to his lips . . . and kisses it, twice. It sweeps me off my feet. If he weren't holding on to me, I would fly away like one of those lovers in a Chagall painting.

Mick lowers my hand but is still holding on to it. "Why are you actually going back to New York?" he wants to know.

The question catches me off guard. *Why am I actually going back to New York?* For a moment I don't have an answer. In fact, two, three, ten moments later, I still don't have one.

"Molly?" he says.

"I'm not sure. I felt . . . lost. I didn't fit in. I wasn't connected."

Strange how I use the past tense. *I felt lost. I didn't fit in. I wasn't connected.* And now?

"Too bad," says the gentle giant.

Mick is leading the way. Alexanderplatz is crowded. We turn right, go down steps, enter an area with various exits, tunnels, stairs, and escalators. We turn right again. Go up steps. And there's the walkway and the leather shop.

"Can you get two subway tickets? At the fare box?" Mick asks me, pointing to a box where four people are standing. He gives me 40 East pfennigs. "It'll make things quicker."

The coins feel like play money, so light and flimsy.

I line up. Through the shop window, I see Mick talking to a man. Mick turns to me, gives me a thumbs-up, and then I lose him behind a post.

There are two women in front of me at the fare box. I watch the first one throw coins into the box then turn a handle and out comes a ticket. That doesn't look too hard. I watch the second woman do it too. But she takes a ticket without throwing in money and starts away.

"I saw that!" says a man behind me to the woman. "You didn't pay!"

"Mind your own business!" the woman growls, and then disappears down the steps.

It's my turn now. I throw the coins into the box and catch a glimpse of Mick walking through the store with the shopping bag. *Lucky again!* goes through my head as I turn the handle on the fare box. The machine seems so primitive, like a Fisher-Price cash register in a nursery school classroom. Just as I pull out the strip with tickets, a shrill female voice near the leather shop breaks through my thoughts: "Hello! Perfect timing!" My back is to the door, but I'm thinking that that voice sounds vaguely familiar. "I just got here. You, too?" says the voice.

Every centimeter of me goes into shock. I whip around. And there she is: Pretty in Pink herself, Carlotta Schmidt, with her pink tube dress, her black patent boots, her black leather aviator jacket. And she is talking to *Mick*. To *my* Mick. To the Mick who just kissed my hand. Twice. To the Mick I wanted to invite to Thanksgiving dinner. Mick as in Jagger.

"Whew! I'm glad I'm not late," Carlotta says, looking at her watch. "We did say two fifteen, didn't we?"

"Uh, yeah," says Mick. "Right."

"So, where to first? The TV tower? The Museum Island?"

Mick looks at me. Carlotta sees him look at someone and turns to me. "Hey, Molly Moo! What are *you* doing here?"

I'm in worst-case-scenario mode. My breathing is shallow. My heart is palpitating. My ears are buzzing. If I weren't paralyzed in place by the shock, I would swoon.

"Do you know each other?" Mick says, perplexed. "You're friends?"

I am stuck. Stuck, stuck, stuck. I am a piece of wood stuck under a door, jammed into a crack, wedged between two walls.

"We go to school together!" says Carlotta.

Mick turns to me. He is truly baffled. "Were you in the S-Bahn together?"

"No. We just happened to be sitting in the same car," says Carlotta. Her voice is as shrill as the color pink. She talks to him, babbling on and on: "But what were you doing with Mol— Oh, I get it! You were bridging the time with her. Until two fifteen."

Bridging the time with her? Was Mick *using* me to pass the time until he could meet Carlotta? Is *that* why he picked me up at the Intershop? So he wouldn't have to wait all by himself? Is *that* why he wanted to have lunch? So he'd have something to do for two hours? Maybe he left those Legos in the store on purpose so he'd have a reason to go back to Alexanderplatz. Is *that* why he told me to go on ahead to Greifenhagener Strasse? So he could go and meet her?

I feel . . . what? Devastated? Yes! How could I be so wrong about someone—*again*?

What a lousy bastard! What a skunk!

But is he really? Is it possible?

"I thought you were going shopping!" Carlotta says to me.

I turn to Mick. "You had a date with her?" My voice is going to crack. I focus all my energy into forcing myself not to cry. Please, don't let me cry in front of Carlotta, not in front of Mick who has just . . . just what? Just broken my heart, goddamn it! My heart! That's exactly what it feels like.

Mick is tottering on a dangerous line. "Yes . . . ," he says to me. "We . . . agreed to meet, but then . . ." He looks at Carlotta. "I was . . . going to . . . but then—"

"But *then*?" I shout.

It's the story of my life: *But then.* I was happy. But then my mother died. I was happy. But then Oliver Pollen dumped me. I was happy. But then we moved to Berlin. And then the Wall fell and I met that lousy bastard Mick as in Jagger.

"But then? But then *what*?" I shout at Mick. "What?"

He takes a step toward me, but before he can even open his mouth to answer, I'm history. There's no way I will stand here and listen to him tell me what his "what" is. Never!

Fifteen

The Red Shoes

I know I'm not going the right way. But I don't care. If I get lost, I get lost. It's too hard to think now, too hard to concentrate on where I'm going, too hard to ask for assistance. Besides, even if I knew where to go, I couldn't. The tears are blinding me. Eventually they'll ebb, though, and when I wake up, I'll realize I'm standing in front of the German Federal Pension Fund Office, or its East equivalent, I'll call Fritz, and he'll pick me up. So for now I'll just walk. No, run!

I'm running down a long flight of stairs. My pouch is heavy on my shoulder. It bangs against my hip, and I feel the chisel and the hammer through the leather.

I arrive in a huge mint-green hall with high ceilings and one, two, no: three levels connected by cascading staircases. To the right of me is one track, to the left three. On the walls it says "ALEXANDERPLATZ," but I don't think I've ever been here. It's not the subway line that took us to Pankow, it's not the S-Bahn, it's certainly not a ghost station, so what is it?

I walk along the platform, away from Mick and Carlotta, to the far end of the station and then up a flight of stairs. At the top I turn back around and read the sign. Aha. That was the train to Hönow. I'm on a middle level, and I can look all the way down into the station. If I weren't so miserable, I might find the architecture elegant. But I'm miserable. Mick used me. He was careless. He was pretending to enjoy himself, and all the time he was just looking at his watch, just waiting until he could meet up with Carlotta Schmidt.

I'm riding up an escalator now. I land at another level. There aren't very many people here. In fact, there's no one here. In front of me is a long tunnel. A really long and dimly lit tunnel. And it stinks. Suddenly, I'm smelling everything again. For a while back there, with Mick, I was only aware of the cedar. *His* cedar. But now I smell the disinfectant again. Everywhere. And that piss puddle over here and the beer that someone spilled over there. Cigarette butts. Mold and—oh! Footsteps. They're behind me. I'm afraid to turn around and look. Up ahead, I feel the cold air from the end of the tunnel. I hear the sound of traffic and the laughter of men. *Whoosh!* I whip around. But there's no one behind me. I turn back and see two men coming toward me. It's scary here. And my pouch is heavy. I want to sit down. I'm tired.

I turn back and retrace my steps through the tunnel. There are lights up ahead. The escalator. I go back down . . . I breathe in through my nose and out through my mouth. My watch tells me it's 2:25. If I concentrate, I will find my way back to the train to Pankow. And if I hurry, I can still fulfill my mission. My mission. Greifenhagener Strasse. My mother's birth house. The wall. A stone. A memory. I will wrap the memory up carefully. And then I will pack my bags. And say good-bye to Berlin. I can do that. I will.

I'm leaning against the balustrade now, looking down again at the station with the trains that go to Hönow and end on Alexanderplatz. People are coming up the steps. Some go up the escalator I just came down, others turn to my right. I follow them. They turn left. I'm right behind them. Then they turn right and go up a flight of steps. I'm at their heels. This is beginning to look familiar. It *is* familiar. It's the platform for the train to Pankow! And there's the newsstand! It's open. I ask for the woman's magazine *Sibylle*. Gwen will be pleased. And then I see a magazine called *Guter Rat*. "Good Advice." It has recipes. Martha will get a kick out of it.

I'm back on track. The subway train moves forward. In eight minutes I'll be at Schönhauser Allee.

I feel lousy. But when I concentrate on the feeling, I think I feel a little less lousy than the lousy I felt fifteen minutes ago. I'm getting used to it. It will become a part of all the other lousys I have felt in my life.

Now that I'm sitting, now that my pulse is back to normal, now that I am not carrying my heavy pouch, now that I can think straight, I am trying to figure out all the other feelings inside me besides lousy. Strangely, it's not so hard sorting it all out. I feel . . . anger. And humiliation. Hurt. Disappointment. Revenge. And . . . and . . . there's something else in there. This one's a little harder to pinpoint than the others. It's floating around inside my fifth dimension, hazy and abstract. It's pushing its way to my consciousness. It feels different than all those other feelings that are weighing me down. This one is . . . light. It's airy. It's bright. It's . . .

Hope.

Hope? Where did it come from?

I let the feeling surface, let it slosh around in me awhile, let it settle in . . . I feel it now. It feels good. It feels warm. It feels right. It has the color of silver. Silver.

It's telling me that maybe I was rash. That maybe I should have stayed to hear Mick's "but then." It's telling me I should trust my feelings. It's telling me I liked Mick. It's telling me he kissed my hand. Twice. It's telling me he really listened when I spoke; he really laughed when I joked. It's telling me that maybe he *did* make a date with Carlotta, but then *he met me.* But then he met me.

It's telling me I should not have run away.

But I did.

And now?

The train stops. We're at Schönhauser Allee.

I walk to the steps that lead down to the street. I faintly hear the sound of a saxophone coming from below. I start down, but then stop. Where am I going again? I sit down at the top of the stairs. I take out my map, unfold it, find the subway stop, follow south along Schönhauser Allee until I get to Stargarder Strasse. And there it is. Greifenhagener Strasse, one block east of Stargarder Strasse, my mother's birth house.

Okay. I can do that.

I get up . . . but then sit back down. I need to figure something out first. It's lurking in my subconscious, nagging at my thoughts. It's a question and it needs to be answered: How do I find Mick?

Maybe I can find the name of Mick's school in . . . where was it again? In . . . Schöneweide? I can ask Edda or Fritz to help. I can call up and give the school my number and ask them to please have Mick get in touch with me. Or . . . maybe I can find Mick's mother in the Birkenwerder telephone book. Perhaps there's a listing for artificial insemination technicians in the Yellow Pages. But do they even have a Yellow Pages in the East? And what's his mother's first name? Do I need her first name? How many Maiers can there be in Birkenwerder who are artificial insemination technicians? . . . I'm sure I can find Mick. And when I do, I'll invite him to visit me in New York. If I find him tomorrow, maybe I can invite him over to eat the Thanksgiving leftovers with me. It always tastes better the second day, anyway. We could— Oh no! What if Carlotta brings him to dinner tonight?

I breathe in through my nose, out through my mouth.

She won't invite him. She has no right. She's not hosting. He won't be there. And maybe, now, she won't come either.

I ban Carlotta from my mind. I conjure back my hope . . . I let it surface again. I let it fill me with its light, silvery brightness.

Who knows? Maybe Mick will try to find *me*. Maybe he's calling the chemistry department at the Free University right this very second to get Fritz's home number. Maybe when I get home, he'll already have called.

But then again, maybe not.

Someone is coming up the steps. *Clickety-click.* A woman in high heels. Behind her I still hear the saxophone. *Clickety-click.* And then she appears. And I see that the she is a he. It's the transvestite with the red shoes! You have to look really hard to see she's a man, but she *is* one, I'm certain. *Clickety-click* go his pretty red shoes as he walks up the steps. At the middle landing, he stops and picks something up off the ground. He looks at it, inspects it from all sides, glances ahead, sees me sitting at the top of the steps, and continues up, *clickety-click.*

"Hello again," he says to me when he gets to the top.

Yes. I'm right. It's a man with a man's voice.

"Hi," I say.

Again I have the strange feeling that I've seen him some-where—before the Senefelderplatz station. But where? Make-up as heavy as his masks. He has made his lips larger by applying lipstick above and below his natural lip-line. He looks concerned. "Are you okay, sweetie?" he says. He speaks German like some kids I know from London. Is he British?

"Thanks," I say. "I'm okay."

"Are you lost?"

Am I lost? "No," I say. "I don't think so." I stand up. For a moment my head spins, feels fuzzy, but I reach out for the banister and steady myself. I wait for the haze to clear, like a fog over Manhattan being burned away by the sun. I feel something give, come undone, pop. If this were a *Twilight Zone*, it would be the moment when I fall back out of the crack and return to our three-dimensional world.

I smile at the man. "No. Definitely not. I know where I am."

I put my map back into my pouch and notice his shoes. They are really beautiful.

"But you lost that adorable tall boyfriend of yours, didn't you?" he says.

"He's not my boyfriend."

"Well, he should be," says the man, chuckling. "He should. He was crazy about you. I know a man smitten when I see one." He opens up his hand. "I just found this on the stairs. It must be yours."

I gasp.

"Go on. Take it." He puts it in the palm of my hand.

It's a Lego mini-figure! The pirate with the red-striped torso and blue hips and legs, but without its head and arms. How did it get here? The last I saw it, it was in the West S-Bahn when the little East German girl in the ski jacket and moon boots gave it to Mick.

"Take it," says the transvestite. Very gingerly he closes my hand over it. And then he grins.

"You have lipstick on your teeth," I note.

"Oh, thank you!" He rubs his teeth and then shows them to me.

I nod my approval.

The train to Otto-Grotewohl-Strasse is arriving.

"Oh, dear!" says the transvestite. "I've got to rush off! Good luck!" He turns toward the train.

"Wait!" I say.

He turns back to me.

"Your shoes. Where did you get those shoes?"

He looks down at his feet. "These? On Nürnberger Strasse. Or Passauer. Somewhere back there in Schöneberg."

I stand, agape. Carlotta was right! That store *does* have nice shoes.

The man winks, then climbs into the train.

I want those shoes. I will find time to buy them tomorrow. I must. I can be flexible if I want to. I can.

Before the door closes, I watch the transvestite open his handbag, take out a newspaper, the *BZ*, and begin to read. Then the doors close and he's gone.

A *BZ*? Oh *now* I know who the man is! He sat opposite me on the S-Bahn from Charlottenburg to Friedrichstrasse! It's the man in the skipper's cap!

Sixteen

The Girl Who Came Out of Her Crack

It's time to go. My mission calls. I slip the mutilated pirate into my coat pocket. I turn back to the staircase, sad, but not despairing, glad, in fact, that life is sometimes stranger than fiction.

As I walk down the steps, the saxophone gets louder and louder. I wonder if—oops! I just stepped on something hard. I look down. Is it possible? It's the left Lego arm! And it fits right into the torso in my hand! My heart begins beating wildly. My eyes scan the steps for the other arm. A few steps down I find the parrot instead, red with green and yellow stripes for feathers. I snap it into the torso's shoulder. This is definitely too strange to be fiction. This is actually *happening*. To me. That silvery feeling starts swirling through me again. Hope, lifting me up, up, up as I go down, down, down. At the bottom of the stairs, a German shepherd is sniffing at something lying on the ground. I grab the pirate's right arm just before the dog raises its hind leg and—

Then I see a Lego brick trail. Yellow. Red. Blue. I'm under the elevated tracks, on the middle island between the east and west side of Schönhauser Allee. I follow the trail west, like Gretel in the woods, picking up the Legos, brick by brick, and slipping them into my bag. The sun is a yellow ball in a cobalt blue sky. Such vibrant color! It's overwhelming. I need some gray, some ordinary Berlin gray. But wherever I look, I'm

131

dazzled by orange, lemon grass, crimson and gold, magenta, green, indigo, and rose. I see a glaring splotch of fire-engine red. An *A* for *Apotheke*. My first East pharmacy.

The saxophonist is just around the corner, under the staircase, his hat on the ground at his feet. It's the man we bumped into at the Pankow subway station. I take another step, and then I see it—the pirate's head. It's the one with the curly black hair, the stubbly chin, and a patch over one eye. It wears a hat with a skull and crossbones. I pick it up and snap it into place. The pirate's almost complete now. Only his sword is missing.

"Ahoy," says a voice.

If this were a movie, I'd call it *The Girl Who Came Out of Her Crack*: "A spellbinding, spine-tingling, life-affirming tale shot in 3D: D-lightful! D-vine! D-sirable!" In this scene, the camera would pull back slowly from the pirate as the saxophone music comes to a crescendo and the two protagonists are revealed: the fifty-foot woman and the gentle giant, their eyes yearning, their lips poised for a kiss, their—

But, wait! This is not a movie. This is my *life*. And this is just *me*, Molly Beth Lenzfeld, standing outside an East Berlin subway station on November 23, 1989. And there's Mick, handing me a tiny little Lego flower. It slips right into the pirate's fist instead of his sword.

I slip the pirate into my pocket as Mick takes a step toward me. He puts his hand under my hood.

"I didn't get the chance before to ask you the third question," he says. "That's why I followed you."

"And what might that be, the third question?" I say, and then hold my breath.

"Is there someone . . . somewhere . . . waiting for you?"

"Waiting for me?"

"You know . . . do you . . . have a boyfriend?"

"Yes," I say, evenly. "Yes, I think I do."

Mick is walking a terrible tightrope between hope and despair. He barely moves, barely breathes when he speaks. "I . . . don't happen to know him, do I?"

"You . . . might," I say.

"Does he have a name?"

"Yes, he does."

Now *he's* holding his breath.

"Mick," I say. "His name's Mick. As in *Maier*."

His relief is absolutely palpable. I am so thrilled for him, so thrilled for me, I want to reach out and hug him. But before I can, he pulls me toward him. Chest on chest. Hip on hip. He has both hands hidden under my hood. We are a hair's breadth away from a kiss.

"Would you like me to help you knock down that garden wall?" Mick whispers.

"I think I can do it myself. But you can watch. And if you like, you can come tonight and help carve the Thanksgiving turkey."

His smile leaps off his face. "I told you!" he says. "I'm the luckiest guy I know!" His eyes caress me a moment. "How did this happen? It's such a mystery."

"A mystery? No it's not," I say. "It's chemistry."

"Chemistry?"

And that's when we kiss.

It's everything it should be. And even more. Because it's not just a promise—it's a yes. A yes with questions still to be answered, but a yes nonetheless.

The saxophone's music embraces us, flows through us, irresistible and bonding. We pull apart for a moment, and Mick holds out his hand. "Would you like to dance?"

Me? Dance? I look around. People are rushing to and fro. It's beginning to snow. "Here?" I say.

"Why not?"

He takes my hand. And this much I know: it feels as if he'll never let it go. Ever.

Thanks!

I started thinking about Berlin and the *Wende*, the amazingly euphoric weeks after the fall of the Wall, at the request of my editor at Rowohlt Verlag, Christiane Steen. She suggested that an all-age novel about the *Wende* might be an interesting project for me. I was skeptical. The *Wende* was, I felt, a purely German subject. I had lived in Berlin many years and knew West Berlin in the 1980s like the back of my hand, but I hadn't been particularly familiar with East Germany or East Berlin, and I was very clearly not German. But the more my editor badgered me about writing this book, the more I racked my brain trying to remember how I had felt and what I had experienced that autumn. I soon realized that I might be able to make the idea work. Therefore, first and foremost, I thank Christiane Steen not only for her excellent editing, but for her patience, determination, and for the very fact that she did not give up on me, even when I said, "*Njet*."

Wallflower is a work of fiction, but from the word *go*, I knew I had to get it right. Tina Kemnitz was the first person I went to in order to find out about young East Germans in the late 1980s. She was eighteen and a first-semester acting student in Leipzig when the Wall fell. I was fascinated by her tales. Much of her experience, optimism, and exuberance became a part of the character Mick Maier.

Florian Lukas, seventeen years old in the autumn of 1989, was my first East German reader. With great élan, he steamrolled through the first draft of my English-language manuscript, giving me great insight into the early years of a future actor and invaluable information about the mind, heart, and times of a Prenzlauer Berg teenager. He made me feel like I was on the right track.

Wallflower embraces several subjects of which I had only fuzzy memories and sometimes little or no knowledge: every-thing from theoretical chemistry to the secret healing power of the *Ketwurst*. The publisher Christoph Links and the artist Susanne Pomerance opened up their address books and put me in contact with some of the experts I needed to talk to.

I owe the authenticity of this book to the people who gave freely of their experience and knowledge in their fields of ex-pertise. After talking to Nicole Wille about what it was like being over six feet tall, I felt Molly Lenzfeld and I understood each other better. Professor Dr. Jörn Manz, head of the De-partment of Theoretical Chemistry at the Free University Ber-lin, was kind enough to spend a few hours in a pizzeria giving me a lesson in Theoretical Chemistry 101. After talking to Siegfried Mattner, I was fairly certain that Mick's mother, an artificial insemination technician, would be the proud owner of a Trabi, one of those tiny East German cars. Ina Brox knew all about Berlin girls with big feet and a limited shoe selec-tion. Dr. Stefan Wolle, director of the DDR-Museum Berlin, took me on a brilliant tour of the Friedrichstrasse train station, reconstructing for me its labyrinth-like border control arena. My heartfelt thanks to all!

The moment I decided to place *Wallflower* in Berlin's S-Bahn and U-Bahn in the year 1989, I knew I was up against a huge community of train enthusiasts who wouldn't hesitate for a second to expose any inaccuracies that might slip into my work. A slew of experts came to the rescue: Andreas Eisen-hart, Ingmar Arnold, Matthias Hiller, Markus Jurziczek, and, first and foremost, the journalist Jan Gympel, who not only answered all of my questions from the color of the leatherette seats on the East S-Bahn to the best way to get lost in the Alexanderplatz station on November 23, 1989, but who also read my early draft and nipped problems in the bud. I am greatly indebted to him for providing me with the critical and intelligent eye of a perfectionist, and for generously handing over facts and information I would otherwise not have had access to.

Heike Barndt, Sabine Berking, Anna Justice, Nicole Kellerhals, Anke Sterneborg, Joya Stindt, and Sabine Ludwig read the work in progress. My thanks for all their constructive criticism.

I would also like to express my gratitude to the intrepid Eva Schweitzer for bringing this book to America, and to Erin DeWitt, who with patience and humor copyedited the occasionally off English of a long-standing expat.

Lastly, I thank the one person who has read, or heard aloud, every single idea and draft for this story: my husband, Eberhard Delius. He has endured hundreds of pages in English and German. I thank him, with all my love.

About the Author

Holly-Jane Rahlens, a born New Yorker, grew up in Brooklyn and Queens and graduated from Queens College. Soon after graduation she moved to Berlin, where she has lived virtually all her adult life. While remaining an American citizen, she has flourished in the German media world, working in radio, television, and film, and creating a series of highly praised one-woman shows. She is the author of six novels: two for adults, two for young adults, and two for all ages. In 2003 *Prince William, Maximilian Minsky and Me* earned the prestigious Deutscher Jugendliteraturpreis as the best young adult novel published in Germany. In 2006 the Association of Jewish Libraries named it a Sydney Taylor Honor Book. It was adapted into the motion picture *Max Minsky and Me,* which has since earned prizes around the world.

Rahlens lives in Berlin with her husband and her adolescent son.

Read more about the author:
www.holly-jane-rahlens.com

Presents:

Winter 2010/Summer 2011 program

www.Berlinica.com

The Berlin Wall Trail provides a tour along the entire length of the infamous Wall that once encircled West Berlin, along the frontline of history in Europe's most exciting city, recounting many of the incidents that have become the legacy of the Wall—whose remnants serve now as a memorial against violence, tyranny, and the abuse of power. The book is published by Esterbauer, Austria, and is sold by Berlinica in the USA.

Michael Cramer moved to the Berlin district of Neukölln as a school teacher in the 1970. He became the Green Party's go-to politician for transportation issues, and a member of the Berlin City Council. Since 2004, he has been a member of the European Parliament. **Peter Trzeciok,** the photographer, is a lifelong Berliner who experienced the Wall from its construction in 1961 to its fall in 1989.

Genre: Travel guide, history
Softcover, 140 pages
Dimensions: 8.5" x 4.75"
Release date: Winter 2010
ISBN 3-85000-147-4
Suggested Retail: $15.95

Biking or hiking on the Berlin Wall Trail is a unique adventure."

—AdventureTravel.com

Berlin in the Cold War vividly describes the conflict between the two superpowers—the USA and the Soviet Union—as it played out in Berlin, the divided city that was the frontier town, the spy post, and the battlefield. The book highlights the events that touched the world: the blockade, the airlift, the uprising of June 1953, the construction of the Wall, stories of escape and espionage, and the fall of the Iron Curtain. Includes many pictures and a map.

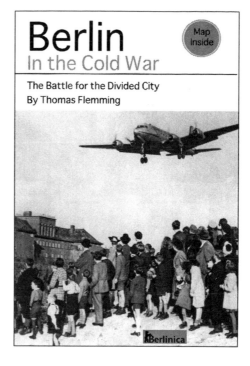

Berlin
In the Cold War

The Battle for the Divided City
By Thomas Flemming

Map Inside

Berlinica

Thomas Flemming is an historian and philosopher who studied at Berlin's Free University. He has written numerous books and newspaper and magazine stories about post-war history, especially in Berlin, and he has curated a number of exhibitions, among them "The History of World War I" at the Deutsches Historisches Museum in Berlin.

"..the whole story of the divided city in just 80 pages."

——Berliner Morgenpost

Genre: Non-fiction, history
Softcover, 80 pages
Dimensions: 6.7" x 9.6"
Release date: Winter 2010
ISBN 978-1-935902-80-5
Suggested Retail: $11.95

Berlin for Young People is the ultimate guide for Berlin visitors, and even for Berliners. The book explains everything you need to know about Berlin's fascinating history and guides your exploration by foot, bike, boat, bus, balloon, riksha, segway, and subway. You'll discover flea markets, bars, and bunkers, learn about museums for currywurst, hemp, antiques, and the GDR, and relax on a beach in mid-city or at a pool on a ship. Includes numerous phone numbers, maps, and a chapter on Potsdam.

Martin Herden, the editor, moved to Berlin in 1981. After studying literature in Berlin, Toulouse and Québec he opened the event agency Herden and the tour operator Herden Studienreisen Berlin. Since 1998 this firm publishes *Berlin for Young People* and provides touristic services: accommodations and guides in all languages.

Genre: Travel Guide
Softcover, 240 pages
Dimensions: 5" x 8"
Release date: Winter 2010
ISBN 978-1-935902-30-0
Suggested Retail: $11.95

"A book full of information and stories—and it even warns you of tourist traps." —Der Tagesspiegel

Berlin for Free is an invaluable guide for the frugal traveler, to everything free in Berlin: Underground pop, classical music, and concerts in the park, art shows and exhibitions, museums and movies, readings and theater, sport events, city tours, gay life, and street fairs. All of these no-cost opportunities for kids and grown-ups alike are neatly arranged and easy to find. The book also includes more than two hundred addresses, phone numbers, and web sites—and all the information is updated.

Berlin for Free

A Guidebook to Music, Movies, Museums and More for the Frugal Traveler

Originally Published by Verlag an der Spree

Berlinica

Monika Maertens, the author, is a student at the Berlin University of the Arts. **Martin Blath,** the original publisher and co-author, came to Berlin in 2002 from the Rhine as a freelance journalist, and also worked in PR. Two years later, he founded Verlag an der Spree—because he loves Berlin, the most exciting city in Europe.

"This book is a worthwhile investment that pays for itself."

—Berliner Kurier.

Genre: Travel Guide
Softcover, 102 pages
Dimensions 5" x 8"
Release date: Winter 2010
ISBN 978-1-935902-40-9
Suggested Retail: $9.95

Edited by Andreas Nachama, Julius H. Schoeps and Hermann Simon

Jews in Berlin

Berlinica

Jews in Berlin: For centuries, Berlin was the center of Jewish life in Germany. Its Jewish citizens strongly influenced the city's cultural life. After World War I, however, economic crisis, hyper-inflation, and depression provided rich soil for the growth of anti-Semitism and ultimately led to the Holocaust. Today, Jewish life and culture are flourishing again. This richly illustrated book depicts Jewish past and present in Berlin.

Julius H. Schoeps (right) is the director of the Moses Mendelssohn Center in Potsdam, the author of numerous books, and claims Moses Mendelssohn among his ancestors. Rabbi Andreas Nachama is the director of the Topography of Terror Museum. Dr. Hermann Simon is the director of the Foundation New Synagogue Berlin and the Centrum Judaicum.

Genre: History, Jewish life
Softcover, 264 pages
Dimensions 6.7" x 9.6"
Release date: Spring 2011
ISBN 978-1-935902-60-7
Suggested Retail: $19.95

"The first comprehensive book about Jewish history, enriched by wonderful illustrations."
—Berliner Zeitung

Berlin Stories shines a light on the Golden Twenties in Berlin, on the cabarets and theaters, the city and its denizens, and the post-World War I struggle between the militaristic Right and the pacifistic Left, which foreshadowed the Third Reich. This book focuses on Tucholsky's newspaper stories and poems about his home town, which he loved and sometimes hated. Some are funny, and some are fierce; they allow a glimpse of the age that shaped the century.

Kurt Tucholsky
Berlin Stories

Journalism from the Golden Twenties

Berlinica

Kurt Tucholsky was one of the most important journalists of the Weimar Republic and wrote for the *Berliner Tageblatt* and *Die Weltbühne*. He was a left-wing democrat, satirist, songwriter, lady's man, poet, and pacifist in the tradition of Heinrich Heine. He ultimately fled the Nazis and committed suicide in exile in Sweden.

"Kurt Tucholsky was one of the most brilliant writers of republican Germany."

The New York Times Obituary

Genre: History, Journalism
Softcover, 155 pages
Dimensions: 5.5" x 8.5"
Release date: Spring 2011
ISBN 978-1-935902-20-1
Suggested Retail: $15.95

The Berlin Wall — Wall Calendar 2011

The Berlin Wall is gone, but there are still remnants to be found, some hidden, some not so hidden, some colorful, some solemn. This 2011 calendar is a collection of 12 photos of the remainders of the Iron Curtain that once divided not only Berlin, but all of Europe.

This calendar can be ordered at
www.cafepress/Berlinica.com
8.5" x 11" $ 22.98
11" x 17" $ 22.98
www.zazzle/Berlinica.com
5.5" x 7" $20/$21
8.5" x 11" $22/$23
11" x 14" $27/$28

prices may vary/
bulk discounts available

Breinigsville, PA USA
25 October 2010
248062BV00004B/11/P